My ~~Lovely~~
Roommate

⌂ I.J Hidee ⌂

My Lovely Roommate
Paperback edition published in 2023
Author I.J Hidee
Copyright © 2023 by I.J Hidee
The moral rights of the author have been asserted.
ISBN 9798387144226

Also Published by I.J Hidee

The Ranking System #1
The Rankless System #2
The Fall of the System #3

● ○ ●

The Class Prince #1
The Prick and His Prince #2

● ○ ●

Y.O.L.O #1

W.O.L.O #2

● ○ ●

Conan the Dandelion #1
Darker Parker #2

● ○ ●

Who Let the Vamps Out? #1
Who Let the Wolves Out? #2

Table of Contents

Prologue

Breaking the Fourth Wall

Jihoon: Uh, Hidee, what are you doing?

Hidee (your very lovely author): Breaking the fourth wall, what do you think? We've got to be original here, make the prologue interesting to catch the readers' attention. Come on, Jihoon, work with me!

Jihoon **narrows eyes**: Who the hell breaks the fourth wall in their prologue?!

No one:

Jihoon:

Hidee: Me c:

Hidee: Let's begin. Your name is Kim Jihoon, right? And you're the main protagonist of the story?

Jihoon: Shouldn't you know the answers? I mean, you *are* the author of the book.

Hidee: I didn't expect to write another main character with so much sass. It's giving me Desmond Mellow vibes.

Jihoon: Des— Who?

Hidee: Oh, haha, uh, no one (*a cookie and pat on the head for those who got the reference ;)*. Ahem, anyway, back to the interview. Can you tell us more about yourself?

Jihoon: I'm a twenty-three-year-old college student majoring in literature and journalism.

Hidee: That's it?

Jihoon: If this book is about me, then the readers will find out about my life struggles.

Hidee: Wow, hold up, things got dark really quick here. I said to *captivate* the readers, not scare them away!

Jihoon: It's not my fault I have a toxic relationship with my roommate.

Hidee **gasps loudly with wide eyes**: You what?

Jihoon: Don't act like you don't know the storyline, you sneaky author.

Hidee: *Shhh*, it's all part of the plan; just go with the flow. So, this toxic roommate of yours. What's his name?

Jihoon: Jax. Jax Bowden. We met back in high school. ***Shivers*** Dark times.

Hidee: What do you mean?

Jihoon: I was bullied. I wasn't openly gay, but everyone knew I wasn't straight, and it didn't help that I was Asian either. It made me the perfect target.

Hidee: How did you handle the racism?

Jihoon: They'd see my facial features and immediately assume I was Chinese—I'm not, by the way. "Ni Hao," they'd say. "Fuck you," I'd answer. So to answer your question, not very well.

Jihoon: But Jax was different. He wasn't nice to me by any means. In fact, he was the worst one out of them. But somehow, he made me feel special. Maybe it was because he was the only person who accepted me for who I was, or because I was lonely and needed someone to lean on, or maybe I was just horny and liked his face—I don't know. But I slowly grew attached to him. Oh, but don't take him for a saint.

Hidee: How would you describe him?

Jihoon: Manipulative, narcissistic, and borderline psychopathic.

Hidee: That's, um, that's a lot of adjectives.

Jihoon: After we graduated, we decided to share an apartment. He studies fashion and design at another university and works part-time as a model. He's quite successful.

Hidee: If he's so manipulative and toxic, why did you move in with him?

Jihoon: It's complicated between us.

Hidee: Complicated?

Jihoon: Yeah.

Hidee: Are you happy with him?

Jihoon looks away and doesn't answer

Hidee: If you're so miserable, why don't you skedaddle out of there and, I don't know, find another roommate that's not so *abusive*?

Jihoon: It's easier said than done.

Hidee: What do you mean? There can't be a rational reason as to why you moved in with your school bully. **narrows eyes**: Are you a masochist?

Jihoon: W-What?! No!

Hidee: Are you in love with him?

Jihoon **smiles sadly**: I guess you'll have to read on to find out.

Chapter 1: The One Night Stand

He pulled my shirt off and pushed me roughly onto the bed, flipping me onto my stomach. He grabbed a handful of my dark hair, turning my head towards him and slamming his lips so hard against mine I could taste a tang of blood. The kiss wasn't as great as I had expected, and that was saying a lot for someone with low expectations. I wasn't asking for sparks and fireworks. But this? This just wasn't it. He fiercely stuck his wet tongue into my mouth. It felt like a muscular eel was trying to worm its way down my throat. Not only was it sloppy and unpleasant, but his saliva tasted strongly of alcohol and tobacco. He finally pulled away and raised my hip. Without warning, I felt something enter me.

"Does it hurt?" the man grunted in a raspy voice. I could hear him breathe heavily behind me. All we did was kiss, and he was gasping for air like he had just run a marathon! I started to regret coming here, but I knew it was too late to back out. Besides, I needed someone to distract me. Someone to stop me from thinking about *him.*

One-night stands had their perks and inconveniences, especially when it was with a stranger. You never knew what kind of person you'd stumble across. It was either a hit-or-miss situation, and I was obviously leaning towards the miss today.

"No, I'm fine," I growled into the pillow.

I'll probably never see this man again. I don't even remember his name. Finkle? Terry? Post Malone? Let's just call him Will.

"Are you okay?" he asked again, but before I could answer, he pushed my face into the pillow to get a better angle inside of me. I gave him a thumbs-up instead. He moved his hips, and I could hear the sound of flesh slapping. My brows furrowed, confused. I thought he was fingering me, but it was actually his erection that he had stuck inside me.

Wait, but why couldn't I feel anything? Was it *that* small? It felt like something short and thick was poking at my butthole. If it weren't for his waist slapping against my ass, I would have thought he'd stuck his pinkie inside me.

This was definitely a miss.

I groaned in despair into my pillow, which "Will" took as a sign of encouragement.

"Oh yeah, you like that, don't you?" I heard him grunt, quickening his pace and continuing... whatever he was trying to do. I felt him lean towards me, his loud grunts just inches away from my ear as he humped. "Your skin is so smooth and pale," he murmured, nibbling on my earlobe. "Such a creamy tone. I could just bite into it."

"No!" I hissed, raising my head and glaring at him. "No bite marks."

He cocked a brow. "Why? Are you not allowed to have bite marks?"

I ran a hair through my messy hair, avoiding his beady eyes. "That's none of your business."

"Do you have a lover?" he asked, slightly annoyed. I didn't answer, and he pushed me onto my back and raised my knees, sticking himself back into me. I waited for the piercing pleasure and pain but felt nothing when he thrust into me. *Nada.* To the point where I wondered if he even entered me.

"You're a dirty boy if you're cheating on someone." He snickered, kissing my neck as he continued to thrust. "I knew you were a slut the second I saw you."

I didn't answer, closing my eyes and deciding to let it slide. I wanted to ask if he could do a better job at making me feel good but asking him to grow a longer dick seemed quite impossible. Besides, the poor man was thrusting and grunting so much, gripping my waist like his life depended on it, it felt wrong to tell him that his efforts were absolutely useless. He repeatedly screamed, "oh, baby," while breaking a sweat, kissing and licking my body while having the time of his life. I sighed mentally. I might as well let him finish.

Meanwhile, my mind started drifting elsewhere, thinking about other things to kill time. The alcohol was starting to wear off, and I tried to remember how I got here in the first place.

>   1.   My roommate, Jax, didn't come back to our apartment. He's been gone for almost a week. He ignored my calls and texts even though I knew damn well he had seen them. He was constantly posting pictures with hot girls on his social media just to rub it in my face, knowing I'd see them.

"Are you feeling it, kid? Oh, I bet you're *really* feeling it," said Will, snickering.

I opened my eyes and immediately regretted it. He was making a nasty face, the one you had right before orgasm. His mouth hung wide open, his eyes tightly shut, and his nose wrinkled as if he were having a seizure—he looked like he had been shot by a bullet and was in agonizing pain. I quickly closed my eyes so I wouldn't have nightmares.

"Yup," I mumbled nonchalantly. "Totally feeling it."

I drifted back into my thoughts.

>   2.   I got annoyed with the silent treatment and decided to do what I always did whenever he didn't give me his attention: get drunk, find a decent-looking stranger, and have a one-night stand to forget about him.

"Come on kid, make some noise. I feel like I'm banging a corpse here," grunted Will, pulling my hair harder. I forced a convincing moan to shut him up.

Now, where was I?

11

3.   I stumbled upon Will in a sketchy bar, somewhere downtown. Everything was blurry after that. I couldn't remember how we started talking, only that we were both very drunk and ready to fuck. He invited me to his house, we drank some more, made out, and well, here we were.

Will wasn't very handsome and nowhere near my type, but he was okay enough for a one-night stand. He looked twice my age, with salt 'n pepper hair and a prickly beard. I normally would go for someone around my age, but I was desperate and horny tonight.

Will interrupted my thoughts again and asked, "Is something wrong?"

Your dick is too small and you're not banging the right place.

"You're doing fine," I mumbled as enthusiastically as I could.

You may wonder why I'm living with a dick named Jax, my narcissistic roommate who is selfish and downright evil. I ask myself the same question every day and still don't have an answer. Feel free to hit me up if you find one for me. But what I can say is that we shared a long and complicated past. I wish we didn't, though. There was nothing pretty about toxic people except their faces.

Jax and I moved in together after graduating high school, but I wouldn't label us as friends. We slept together every now and then, but we weren't sex friends either. Jax and I shared a strange relationship that couldn't be defined. The only word that could describe us was roommates.

Will pulled my face to his and crushed his lips against mine. Another sloppy kiss. I kept my eyes open, glaring at him as he smothered his face against me as if he wanted our bodies to mold into one.

Keep this up and my dick will go soft, I thought to myself. I lowered my gaze and flinched. *Too late.*

I held back a sigh, hoping the torture would end soon. This was a mistake. Coming here definitely wasn't a smart move. More fleeting thoughts flooded my mind.

12

~~I miss Jax.~~
~~I wish he would come back.~~
~~I wish he was with me.~~
~~I want to go home.~~
Roommates.

The rest of the night was a bore, and I pretended to orgasm so Will's pride wouldn't get crushed. Besides, telling him he was terrible and that his dick was two sizes too small would only create more problems. I didn't want to go through the hassle of explaining it to him.

"That was amazing," he panted, removing his condom and plopping onto the bed beside me. I knew he wanted to cuddle the second he wrapped his arms around my waist and touched my hair. I squirmed out of his grasp and pulled myself to the edge of the bed, away from him.

"I'm going to shower," I said, picking up my clothes.

"We can shower together," he suggested, about to get up.

I froze at the idea, quickly letting out a stiff chuckle. "I think it's better if we don't."

He frowned, and I scavenged my brain for a believable excuse. "Give me some time to recover. My body is still sensitive. Besides, I'm not a fan of shower sex. It's dangerous." A pause. "Someone might slip and crack their head."

Hopefully you.

He nodded, giving me a thumbs up. "You're right. Safety first." He plopped onto his back, tucking his arms beneath his head. "I'll wait for you. Don't take too long."

"Mhm."

I picked up my socks and rushed to the bathroom, closing the door and locking it behind me. I pressed my face against my clothes and let out a frustrated scream. I then pulled away, recollected myself, and hopped into the shower. I scrubbed my entire body from head to toe until my skin burned red, trying to wash away the vivid memories of what had happened earlier. I stood under the steaming hot water, the sensation soothing me.

"I'm so stupid," I mumbled to myself. I already knew it, but I needed to hear myself say it. "Stupid, stupid, stupid."

I wouldn't be here if it weren't for Jax. Damn him, why couldn' t he just come home?

After five minutes of scolding myself and cussing out Jax, I finally stepped out of the shower. I slicked my wet hair back and leaned over the sink to wipe away the mist to look at my reflection. I stared into my black eyes as if it was the first time seeing them.

They were as dark as ink, two pristine stones of onyx inside almond-shaped eyes. My lashes were long and thick. People would often tell me I looked too feminine for a boy.

I wiped the fog that started settling on the mirror again, this time focusing on my skin. I was always complimented for having smooth, flawless skin, which I thanked my Asian genes for. I didn't have prominent cheekbones, but I had a nicely curved jawline and was often told I had androgynous features. Unfortunately, it often attracted creeps and got me into messy situations. My eyes didn't wander any lower than my neck. I always avoided looking at my body.

My lips were split open by Will's aggressive kisses, and my eyes widened when I saw a purple bruise on my neck.

"Damn it, I told him not to mark me," I hissed angrily, trying to rub it off. The rubbing only made it worse and irritated my skin. I leaned my hands against the porcelain sink, my head dropping with a tired sigh.

I'll have to hide this from Jax.

I dried up and wiggled into my clothes, tightening my belt around my thin waist. I gave myself one last pitiful look before opening the door. Will was sound asleep, stretched on his bed, still butt naked. He snored so loudly he sounded like he was trying to communicate with aliens from outer space. I scowled, wondering how on earth I ended up sleeping with him.

Oh right, I was drunk.

I decided to take the chance to escape. I headed for the front door, tiptoeing as quietly as I could. Something crumpled beneath my foot, and I froze. I raised my foot and picked up the paper. It was a literary analysis of a Shakespearean play.

I read the first line: *O happy dagger, this is thy sheath.*

I looked back towards Will, wondering if he was a student learning literature. But considering his age, he seemed too old to be a student.

Whatever, it's none of my business. This is the first and last time I'll see him anyway.

I carefully placed the paper back on his desk before grabbing my bag. I twisted the doorknob and left without a proper goodbye.

Chapter 2: A Toxic Relationship

I thanked the driver and got out of the taxi, climbing up the stairs to my apartment. I checked my phone to see if Jax had replied, disappointed but unsurprised to see no new messages. I inserted the key and twisted open the door. My slippers were at the entrance, waiting for me. Having grown up in an Asian household, wearing slippers was a must.

I was planning on staying at Will's place—or whatever the man's name was—but the thought of spending another couple of hours next to his hairy body was a no-go. I flicked on the living room lights, jumping in surprise when I saw Jax sitting on the couch, one leg crossed over the other, reading a fashion magazine he modeled for. His reading glasses framed his indigo-blue eyes and magnified the color of bright cornflowers. I'd seen his eyes more than a million times, but they never failed to captivate me.

Jax had high cheekbones and a perfectly symmetrical facial structure that looked like it belonged to a Greek god. His hair was a dark blond, a copper that looked as rich as gold. I anxiously pressed my lips together at his unexpected presence. What was he doing here? And why was he awake? A thousand questions popped into my mind as I stared at him, and I felt both scared and relieved.

I cleared my voice to break the silence. "Hi," I croaked. "What are you doing here?"

He didn't look up from his magazine. "I live here."

Gee, thanks, Sherlock. That clears everything up.

16

"Where were you? You've been gone for a week." I tried to sound casual and headed to the kitchen for a cup of cold water. I felt dehydrated, probably because of the alcohol, and I needed something to wash down the dryness in my throat.

"I was at my girlfriend's place," he replied nonchalantly, almost making me drop the cup. Hearing that he had a new girlfriend made my chest tighten unpleasantly.

"Girlfriend?" I asked as enthusiastically as I could. Since high school, Jax always had a girl with him. With his face and body, it was easy for him to get girls, but his relationships never lasted. He broke hearts and left them shattered before finding someone else to toy with until he was bored again. Jax only kept people with him for a short time. *"People are temporary,"* he once told me.

He'd look at you so wondrously, so lovingly, you'd think you were his entire world. He'd manipulate you into thinking you were his favorite person, only for you to realize you were nothing but something to kill time. Jax was only interested in temporality, which hurt many people, including me.

"You have a new girlfriend?"

Jax finally looked up, a sly smile pulling the corners of his lips. "Does it bother you?"

"Why would it bother me?" I muttered coldly. One day he was with girl A, the next day with girl B, and before you knew it, he was with girl C. There weren't alphabets to count the number of women he'd been with.

He shrugged, saying, "You always make that face when you're jealous."

I opened my mouth to protest, but his gaze caught mine.

"I think it's cute."

My face reddened, and I quickly turned around, angrily chugging the cup of water.

Cute? Who the hell is he calling cute?! And what's up with that smirk on his face?

17

I was so caught up in my train of thought that I drank too quickly and choked on the water. I coughed violently and hit my chest. Jax joined me in the kitchen.

"Do you need help?"

"I'm fine," I muttered weakly, wiping the water from my lips.

"I thought you'd be used to gagging by now." He smiled innocently, his crystal blue eyes glistening with amusement. I always hated that look, the one stained with fatuous superiority. "Isn't that what bottoms do? Gag?"

I shot him a glare. "Leave me alone," I spat.

He raised his shoulders. "You're right. Why should I care about your gay activities? You're always whoring yourself out anyway," he mused, his harsh words causing me to flinch.

"I don't sleep with that many men."

He grabbed my arm and pulled me dangerously close to him. He sniffed my shirt, his nose wrinkling. With a condescending tone, he growled, "You reek of alcohol."

My body froze when I witnessed something flash through his eyes. The intensity in his gaze translated with pure displeasure. He was angry. Jax roughly grabbed my chin, his fingers tightening around my jaw as he lowered his gaze to my lips, which was when I remembered Will had left a cut on my lower lip when he kissed me.

Jax cocked a brow and grimaced, his gaze turning as sharp as an icicle. "You're fucking disgusting, you know that?" He yanked down my collar, his eyes wandering towards the side of my neck. "Even got yourself a hickey."

I felt heat rise up my collarbone and quickly pushed his hand away. Jax always pointed out how I was sleeping with other men, but he was always sleeping around with other people too. Just because they were women didn't make him any better. And if he hated homosexuals so much, why did he agree to move in with me? Despite knowing this man for years, he was a complete mystery.

"If I'm so disgusting, why don't you go back to your girlfriend?" I demanded, raising my voice.

"Because I missed you, Jihoon."

His smooth, sweet words made me stiffen. Despite the flutter in my chest, I knew it was a lie. Jax's words were nothing but twisted lies. He stepped closer, his height casting a long shadow over me. He studied my face and I felt exposed and vulnerable under his gaze.

"Did you miss me that much?" His voice was softer, gentle almost.

I stared at my slippers. I felt like a kid scolded by his parent. There was nothing to be embarrassed about. I hadn't done anything wrong, but for some reason, I couldn't look him in the eyes.

My voice was no more than a whisper when I said, "You weren't answering my calls."

He carefully brushed a strand of hair away from my forehead. "Did that bother you?"

I felt like I was being babied and blushed furiously, yet some part of me was excited that he was giving me his attention. It was pathetic. "Yes."

"Did you miss me?" He already knew the answer.

"No."

"Look me in the eyes when you speak."

I bit my lower lip before locking eyes with him. His dangerous blue eyes were beautiful, both terrifying and vicious. Then again, the brightest creatures were always the most toxic.

"Yes," I finally whispered, telling the truth, which made Jax smile. "I missed you. I hate it when you're not here. I hate being alone. I don't like eating alone and I worry about you, and—"

Jax pushed his lips against mine, cutting me mid-sentence. My eyes widened, and I tried to pull away, but he knew me too well and knew my reaction wasn't honest. I quickly gave in, my arms circling around his neck as I stepped on my toes, desperate for more. The contrast between Will's kiss and Jax's was obvious. Jax knew how to make me feel good, and he definitely knew how to use his tongue.

Now, this was a real kiss.

He became more and more demanding as our tongues mingled and swirled. He pulled me onto the counter, and I wrapped my legs around his strong torso, getting lost in the warmth of his touch. He started unbuttoning my shirt, and I pulled away, gasping for air.

"Promise me you won't leave again," I blurted.

He gave me a reassuring smile, removing my shirt down my shoulders. "I would never," he whispered, kissing my forehead.

"Promise me," I begged nonetheless. He leaned closer, his lips almost touching mine.

"Oh baby, you know I don't make promises."

He started undoing my belt, and I let his hands explore my body. I was grateful for Jax, grateful he spared time for me. Grateful he gave me his attention. Grateful he kissed and touched me despite my sexuality. Grateful for living with me despite how filthy and disgusting I was. Despite having endless models and beautiful women to sleep with, he always came back to me. Perhaps not immediately, but eventually, he would. And that made me feel so *fucking* special.

He put his hands on my knees and pried them apart, making me blush madly.

He nibbled on my lip, growling, "This is mine."

My heart pounded as he regarded me with an intimate, possessive gaze that made me feel alive.

Jax and I weren't dating. No official title labeled us. We weren't bound by promises, commitments, or responsibilities. We shared an unappealing, shallow relationship. What were we? We were roommates.

***

I was in Jax's bed when I woke up the next day. My clothes were scattered on the floor, and there were used condoms in the trashcan. I sat up, my entire body tired and sore. When I turned to my side, Jax was gone.

Chapter 3: A Manipulative Roommate

I didn't know why I believed Jax or why I was always disappointed in his repetitive behavior. He wouldn't change. I knew he wouldn't. But my expectations were blinded by hope. Knowing him, he had probably gone to see his new girlfriend. I fell asleep again until my alarm went off, and I let out an annoyed groan, blindly searching for my phone.

Come on, Jihoon, get up. You have class today. Come on, you can do it, you can…

I drifted asleep, only to be awakened by the second alarm I set for safety.

DRINGGGG. DRINGGGG. DRINGGG.

I turned off my backup alarm and pressed my face against my pillow, letting out an annoyed groan.

Come on, you can do it. You have to get up this time or you'll be late. I BELIEVE IN YOU. YOU CAN DO IT! YOU CAN….

I fell asleep a third time, but when my third alarm went off, I forced myself to get up, knowing there wouldn't be a fourth. I fought the urge to fling my phone out the window and got out of bed, putting on my slippers. But as soon as I stood, I yipped. A sharp pain jolted up my waist.

It still hurt. I waited a few seconds and counted up to ten, waiting for the pain to disappear. I took a deep breath, taking another step forward. I limped to the bathroom like an old man. My face hardened when I saw my reflection in the mirror. My hair was a mess and looked like a bird's nest, but that wasn't what made me scowl. I traced a finger under the purple bruise beneath my eye before letting my finger fall to my split lips. My gaze wandered to my torso, my muscles turning tense at the fresh bruises patched over my skin. From experience, I knew they'd mar into an uglier color. I turned my face to the side and frowned at the injury near my ear.

Jax never knew when to draw the line, and he definitely crossed it last night. I ran a hand through my hair, trying to recall everything that had happened, but I could only remember passing out from both exhaustion and pain. My eyes fluttered open as I glared at myself.

"Why does he always have to be so rough?" I muttered, my voice raspy. My throat still ached, and it wasn't because I had just woken up.

I spared myself from examining the rest of my body. I knew it wasn't going to be pretty. I washed up and quickly put on a clean pair of clothes: long jeans and long sleeves to cover up the evidence. As for my face, I used a concealer I had bought in a drugstore, a trick that Jax taught me so no one would ask about my injuries. *Injuries heal. Everything will be fine.*

After giving myself some pep talk, I went to the kitchen for breakfast. My eyes widened when I saw Jax. He was having his morning coffee. The morning sun peeked through the glass window, shining over his beautiful skin and brightening the depth of his eyes. He was wearing a white knitted sweater, his sleeves slightly pulled up, revealing the veins in his strong arms. His beautiful blond hair looked soft and silky like summer clouds. All I could think of was how unfair it was for someone so cruel and vicious to look so divine and angelic. His bright eyes flickered towards me, and I almost flinched. My cheeks lit on fire, and I dropped my gaze.

"You're up?" he asked, his husky voice resonating in my ears. "I was about to wake you."

"I'm not a kid. I can get up myself," I snapped angrily, walking past him and grabbing the box of cereal. I tried not to wince at each footfall, keeping the expression on my face as calm and composed as I could. Deep down, I was fueling with anger, but I didn't want to make a scene so early in the morning. Who knew what he'd do to me if I misbehaved?

"Really?" He snorted. "Is that why you put on three alarms every morning and complain to me when you forget to put on a fourth?"

"That was one time!"

"Once a week," he corrected with a gentle smile, clearly amused.

I averted my gaze, grumbling, "Whatever."

He watched as I poured cereal into my bowl. I added milk and shoved a spoonful into my mouth, ignoring his lingering gaze.

"Aren't you going to sit?" he inquired.

"You're asking too many questions."

My ass still hurt, so sitting down wasn't a good idea. I turned to finish breakfast in my room but let out the tiniest whimper when I stepped forward. It was a small, soft noise, but Jax noticed. He looked at me carefully before saying, "I didn't mean to be so rough that night." He almost sounded apologetic. If he wasn't such an ass, I would have believed him. "I got excited, and you were just too cute."

I looked down at my slippers and contemplated throwing them at him. But he continued, his melodic voice making my boiling anger fall to a simmer. "It's been a while since I've seen you naked." My cheeks reddened, but my anger spiked again when he said, "The other girls I've been with were such a bore," he went on as if it was a legitimate excuse for being abusive.

"Do you beat the women you sleep with too?" I seethed, but I already knew the answer. Jax was only violent towards me. He acted like a total saint in front of others! He'd act like the perfect boyfriend who bought his girlfriend chocolate and roses, but he was the Devil himself with me. Anyone sane and rational wouldn't go anywhere near him, but I wasn't sure if that said more about him or me.

"Why do you even sleep with women if they bore you?" I sighed.

"For their boobs and ass, why else?" he said with an elated grin etching his lips as if it was the most obvious answer.

"How romantic," I scoffed.

"But I much prefer hearing your moans in bed."

"And you call yourself straight," I snorted sarcastically.

Jax's smile vanished, and my heart thudded with fear. I stiffened when he stood up and walked towards me, my heart pounding terribly inside my chest. Jax hated when I implied that he could be anything other than straight. I knew better than to joke about his sexuality. Jax was straight, period.

He raised his hand, and I flinched, waiting for him to hit me. I opened my eyes when his fingers wrapped around my jaw, pulling me closer to him. Jax turned my face to the side, knowing the exact spot he had hit me last night.

"Good, you covered it up. Does it hurt?" He gently pressed his thumb against it, and I winced.

"Ouch! Don't touch it. You'll wipe off the makeup."

He studied my face with an expression I couldn't read. "I wonder what your parents would think if they knew you were still sleeping with men."

My chest tightened.

"They'd be disgusted," he replied for me, his fingers sinking into my jaw as I stared at him.

"You're worse."

He smiled easily. "At least I sleep with women."

Jax was right. At least *he* was straight.

Jax 1, Jihoon 0.

"You should stop aiming at my face," I muttered under my breath, changing the subject. "People might find out and start asking questions. Besides, I hate putting on makeup. The concealer has a mucky texture."

"Your one-night stand was allowed to leave a mark on you, but I can't?"

My eyes fluttered in surprise. Jax almost sounded jealous, and I felt my heart get excited over his possessiveness. It made me feel like I was worth something, and as much as I hated the feeling, I was secretly happy.

"Yeah, well, thanks to you, I won't be sleeping around with anyone for a while."

"That was the point."

Jax smiled and finally let me go, leaning against the counter with his strong arms crossed over his firm chest. He tilted his head, his eyes never leaving mine. He looked at me with his sinful eyes, and the myriad shades of blues swirling in his pupils drew me in. To say his eyes were blue was like saying the sun was yellow— sufficient but lacking. They generated a feeling inside me that I couldn't explain.

"Does the rest of your body hurt?"

"Like you care," I laughed humorlessly.

"I've always cared, Jihoon." He sighed, looking at me with those tragically beautiful eyes. "I always care if it's you."

Lies, lies, lies, lies. I kept repeating inside my head, but my stomach did somersaults. I wanted to avoid having expectations for someone who could never fulfill them, but my emotions wouldn't obey, and once again, I was swayed by his empty words.

"My manager is busy this afternoon, so he can't drive me home after my photoshoot. Will you pick me up?"

"You can drive yourself."

"It's a photo shoot for a famous alcohol brand, and I'll probably be drinking."

"I have a project to finish."

But Jax tossed something towards me, and I quickly caught it. They were his car keys.

"I finish at three. Don't be late."

My grip tightened around the keys, my eyes flickering to him. "Jax—"

He left.

26

"Great," I muttered under my breath. "Beat me to a pulp and treat me like a slave, why don't you?"

It's time for you to man up, Jihoon. Stop letting Jax use and step all over you. You're better than that. That's right, you deserve better.

I was about to run after him to tell him I couldn't pick him up, but I stopped at the door when I saw something on the counter. I opened the white paper back, my brows pulling together at the ointment and creams. There was a small note written in Jax's fancy handwriting.

For your injuries.

My heart fluttered, and I bit my lower lip. A sad smile grew on my lips, followed by a pathetic chuckle as my heart was filled with joy. Hopeless. I was absolutely hopeless.

Chapter 4: Tough Love

I left the apartment and took the bus to university, but the moist and stuffy atmosphere made my nose wrinkle as soon as I stepped inside the vehicle. It was crowded. I apologized as I squeezed past them but didn't get very far and ended up wedged in the middle. I looked around. All the handholds were taken. While I stood there, squished between two people like a sandwich, I stared out the window and couldn't help but think about what happened last night and this morning with Jax. Despite all the terrible things he put me through, my mind had the toxic habit of filtering and keeping only the good memories, like how he bought me ointment for my injuries—everything else became minor details.

He cared.

I shook my head.

No, if he truly cared, he wouldn't have hurt you in the first place.

The bus made a turn to the left, and everyone shifted. The man standing behind me pressed against me. "Sorry," he apologized in a gruff voice, his lips a bit too close to my ear to my liking.

I turned towards the old man and forced a wry smile. "It's okay," I said. His chest was pressed against my back. I thought that maybe there were just too many people on the bus, but my body stiffened.

Was this man actually grinding against me?!

I snapped my head towards him, his face inches away from mine. I could feel his hot breath against the nape of my neck, quick and short, almost panting as he rubbed himself against me. I could feel his boner rub against the seam of my pants.

"What the hell?!" I hissed, trying to move away from him. But there were too many people, making it impossible for me to escape. The bus curved again, allowing the man to push harder against me. He moaned into my ear, gasping a "fuck" when his crotch pushed against me. "You feel so good."

His hands tightened around my waist as he continued to grind against me like a dog in heat, moaning into my ear so low and quiet that only I could hear. Everyone else had their earphones on and were too busy staring at their phones to notice.

Repulsed, I snarled, "Get off me before I bite your dick!"

"Please do," he groaned, making me want to puke. "Asians are so sexy."

My hands balled into fists, and I was about to slam my foot against his, but he suddenly whispered something into my ear, "You like this, don't you?" He cackled. "You're so disgusting."

"You're disgusting, you know that, right?" Jax's words echoed inside my mind, making me turn rigid. I felt him grind harder; he was basically fucking me at this point. My mind went completely blank, and my body grew numb. I knew what was going on, but it was as if I couldn't feel it anymore, the will to fight back suddenly vanishing like candlelight under a gust of wind.

"Disgusting, disgusting, disgusting, disgusting..." Jax's voice mockingly chanted inside my mind. My teeth sunk harder into my bottom lip, my nails digging into my palms. I hated this so much, but my body wouldn't move. They were right. I *was* disgusting. But it wasn't my fault, right? I couldn't help the way I was. I swallowed hard.

The stranger's fingers were inches away from my crotch, but I kept my mouth shut. But someone suddenly yanked his hand away from me, stepping between us to shield my body with his.

"Wow, I didn't know people filmed pornos here," said the teasing voice.

My eyes widened when he spoke loud and clear for everyone to hear, the hint of amusement catching their attention. The old man flinched, gritting his teeth before quickly pushing past the crowd to get off the bus. I blinked a few times, feeling my muscles relax. The fog clouding my mind finally started to clear up, and the taunting voices also disappeared. I then realized that the guy who saved me was staring at me. He was tall, maybe two heads taller than me but a few inches shorter than Jax.

His chestnut-brown hair reflected the morning sunlight as did his eyes, warm amber swirls with strands of green and gold in the center. They held something so naturally beautiful and decadent, I couldn't take my eyes off him.

"Are you okay?" he asked, breaking the silence with a voice threaded with curiosity. He gave me a worried smile.

"Yeah," I lied, my throat feeling dry. He studied my eyes, and as if he could see right through me, he gently murmured, "You should say something when you're not okay." My heart raced. "And for what it's worth, I don't think you're disgusting."

I was so taken aback that I turned my head around without a thank you. I wasn't used to getting flustered by someone other than Jax.

He stood behind me for the rest of the ride. His body was big and strong enough to keep a few inches between us to avoid making me feel uncomfortable, which surprised me considering how little space there was to begin with. It was finally my stop, and half the crowd got off, including the guy who saved me.

He must be a student too, but before I could thank him, a line of people separated us. I wanted to call out his name but realized I didn't know it. I frowned, watching him cross the road and join his friends, disappearing around the next block.

Maybe next time.

Someone suddenly put their arm around me. Lola greeted me with a wide grin, her shoulder-length brown hair neatly tucked behind her ear, revealing her many silver earrings around her ear lobe. She had a doll-like face, cute and small, with slightly plump lips that dropped when upset. Lola had a petite figure, and I always thought she was more beautiful than average. I would have a crush on her if I were straight. Though, her looks contrasted with her boyish personality.

"What happened to your face?" She scowled, her smile disappearing in a flash as she leaned closer to me. "Is that a bruise?!"

"I bumped into a wall," I mumbled, pulling away.

But she knew me too well and angrily asked, "It was Jax again, wasn't it?" She started pulling up her sleeves at my silence, looking like she was ready to brawl. "Alright, where is that bitch? I'm going to throw some hands. No one hurts my baby Jihoon!"

I rolled my eyes, gluing her hands back to her sides. "No one is throwing anything. Just forget it. It doesn't hurt that much," I said, offering no more information.

She frowned.

"He apologized," I lied. Making up excuses for Jax felt repulsive, but I knew Lola would never let it go if I didn't. "He bought me some ointment."

Lola put her hands on my shoulders and started shaking me back and forth. "That doesn't make it okay!" she said loudly, catching the attention of some of the by-passers. "He's abusive and is always finding ways to hurt you, stomping on you like you're a cockroach while you treat him like a king." My eyes narrowed at how dramatic she sounded. And did she just compare me to a cockroach?

She plastered her hands on my cheeks and my lips puckered like a puffer fish. "WAKE UP, JIHOON! YOUR ROOMMATE IS A MANIPULATIVE, PSYCHOPATHIC SADIST!"

The sad part was I was already aware of that.

"OPEN YOUR EYES, DUDE," she cried. "AND I MEAN THAT IN THE LEAST RACIST WAY POSSIBLE!"

I pulled away from her grasp. "Speaking of toxic people, remind me who's the one who got cheated on last week?"

Lola gasped, her voice lowering to almost a growl. "Oh, you did *not* just go there."

Fwop, fwop, fwop, she beat me up with her lady bag, and I apologized for crossing the line. My body wasn't really in the best state to be getting beaten up right now.

"I guess we can both agree that we'll be single for a while," she sighed, blowing a strand of hair away from her face. "You and

I are on the same boat, buddy. Screw these toxic hoes. Let's go out for drinks Friday night. I need some alcohol in my system."

"I'm busy," I croaked.

"I'll pay."

"What time?"

"You heartless bastard," she sighed, shaking her head. "I'll text you the details later. I'll ask my friends if they want to come too. Let's cross our fingers that they bring cute guys."

"You sure you want a cute guy seeing you drunk?" I asked, remembering how she was tripping over nothing and strip-dancing to Ed Sheeran the last time she was drunk. Didn't think that was possible? Me too, but Lola proved me wrong. "Your ugly crying might scare them off."

Her mouth widened, and she slapped my arm. "I do *not* ugly cry!" she protested. I pulled out my phone and scrolled through my gallery, showing her all the pictures I had taken when she was ugly crying. She almost beat me to a pulp, and by the time we made it to our building, I felt like I had more bruises than when I first left the house.

Tough love, right?

Chapter 5: My Savior

Jax and I met in high school when I was at the lowest point in my life. I always believed that it was because he was there at a specific time that I grew attached to him—that if I was still here today, it was thanks to him. You see, I had always been the odd one out. My older brother and sister were straight-A scholar students who graduated with full scholarships. My brother was a lawyer, and my sister was studying to become a surgeon. They were the perfect, ideal children that most Asian parents wanted. Compared to them, I was always lacking. I wasn't a troublesome child, but I was never good enough. My parents said hurtful things and lowered my self-esteem until I had none left, driving us apart. My bad relationship with my parents made it impossible for me to come out of the closet. I eventually accepted the fact that they'd never accept who I was and gave up on the hope of being loved. Home was hell, but school was worse.

7 years ago
Murmurs and whispers spread throughout the classroom as soon as I stepped in. My eyes widened, my body stiffening as I saw the insults scribbled all over my table in permanent marker.

Faggot, chink, slut, man whore...

I felt my stomach lock tight, my head buzzing with anger and embarrassment. I looked up, and my classmates turned away, avoiding my gaze while muffling their laughter and sharing snickers. The professor stepped in, and everyone fell quiet, rustling around as they went to sit in their seats.

I was the only one who was still standing.

"Is something wrong, John?" asked my Math professor, Mr. Trenton. More snickers.

"It's Jihoon, sir," I whispered as the students burst into laughter.

"Right, is there something wrong?" he asked in a slightly irritated voice, annoyed that I had corrected him. "Why aren't you sitting down?"

Everyone glared at me, the suffocating atmosphere making it hard for me to breathe. I clenched my trembling hands and felt my nails sink into my palms.

"Nothing's wrong," I mumbled, but Mr. Trenton saw my table's state and furrowed his brows. He looked like he was about to say something but stopped.

"We'll talk about this once class ends," was all he said before starting roll call. I pulled out the chair and sat down, glancing at my table one last time before turning towards the window, avoiding the smirks and smug looks on my classmates' faces.

Die faggot.

The bell rang.

Class ended, and I collected my things, following the professor to his office, but as I left the classroom, my eyes locked with one of the students who sat at the very back. Jax gave me a sardonic grin, mouthing one word before I broke our gaze.

"Die."

I entered the professor's office, and Mr. Trenton sank into his chair while I stood before him, staring at his chest while I waited for him to say something.

"Have you been bullied like this in middle school?" he asked, finally breaking the silence. I didn't answer. Mr. Trenton ran a hand through his non-existing hair before crossing his arms over his chest. "Do you know who wrote those things on your table?"

Jax and his friends.

I shook my head, but that only upset Mr. Trenton even more.

"I can't help you if you don't tell me the truth," he said with a frown. But even if I told him the truth, I doubted he'd be able to help me.

"John— I mean, Jin," he began. "If you don't tell me anything, I'll ask the students myself."

"No!" I blurted with wide eyes.

A dreadful silence broke through the air, and his eyes strained slightly as he looked at me. Mr. Trenton took in a deep breath. "Jin, have your parents ever considered taking you to a therapist?"

My nails sunk deeper into my skin, and I wondered if I was bleeding. "There's nothing wrong with me," I said faintly, but the look on his face told me he thought otherwise. I took a sharp breath, swallowing the lump in my throat, "There's nothing wrong with me."

"Jin," he murmured, looking at me the way any adult would with a teenager.

"Jihoon," I corrected quietly, but he didn't hear me.

"Some people become really sad at a young age, which can be due to many factors and sometimes none at all. I think you need help."

Help for what? For being myself?

I returned to my classroom after being lectured. The rest of the day went by like any other. When the last bell rang, everyone picked up their things and left the classroom to go home. The classroom progressively emptied until I was completely alone. I waited a few more minutes before getting up, leaving my bag where it was. I didn't go down the stairs but went up to the rooftop, and a gentle gust of wind greeted me when I opened the metal door. I walked to the unprotected ledge, taking in a shaky breath.

Up here, I felt like I could see the world. I saw the trees, the flowers, and the cheerful students leaving the school gates with wide smiles as they headed home. I walked closer towards the edge until the tips of my toes were no longer beneath solid ground. I felt the color in my face drain down my neck. It suddenly became harder to breathe, yet I had never felt so alive. It was like standing on a diving board, ready to be greeted by the cold, harsh water below. Adrenaline pumped through my veins. I bent my shaky knees and took a shaky breath as I squeezed my eyes shut.

Die.

But my body wouldn't budge. As much as I wanted to end my life, I was scared. I staggered back, taking as many steps as possible until my legs gave up. I stumbled to the ground, bursting into sobs. Tears spilled uncontrollably down my face while my lips and chin quivered. I grasped at the concrete for reassurance, sobbing.

"For a second there, I thought you were going to jump," said a voice.

My eyes widened, and I turned around. Jax stood at the door, leaning against the doorframe. His eyes burned an icy blue, with an almost bored and disappointed expression on his face. I scrambled onto my wobbly feet, wiping away my tears while holding back the whimpers.

"Are the rumors of you being gay true?" he asked bluntly. "You always look at me the way girls do."

I didn't answer, and he laughed. "Wow, so you really like guys."

"Jax—"

He grimaced, disgust filling his beautiful eyes. "Gross, you even know my name. No wonder you were about to jump." My lips parted at his cruel words. "Why'd you change your mind?"

Speechless at first, I tried to collect myself, "That's none of your business."

His voice or eyes showed no remorse when he said, "If you want to die so bad, you should jump. I heard that death isn't too bad. Here, why don't I help you?"

My body froze when he came closer. He pushed me back, and I staggered from the impact, getting closer to the ledge.

"Wait," I stuttered, quickly dodging his hand as he tried to push me again. But he gave me another hard push until I was one step away from falling. I glanced behind me, my stomach twisting into knots and my palms clammy as soon as I saw how high we were. He was about to give me one last push, but I grabbed his arm, sinking my nails into his skin while I held onto him for my dear life.

"Stop it!" I begged.

"It's not like anyone's going to care anyway. Wimps like you annoy me the most," he muttered, his glacier eyes glaring at me. "Victims who cry and whine about how life is unfair. Cowards who choose death because they think it's easier. People like you are the most selfish beings to exist. You think that you're the only one who has it rough?" he demanded.

My eyes widened. "No!"

"Do you think you weren't meant to live?" he shouted, trying to uncurl my fingers from his arm. There was so much anger and hatred in his eyes. "You think you're that worthless?"

"I wasn't thinking!" I sobbed, tears streaming down my face. "Jax, please stop!"

I was going to die. I was really going to die.

"Stop what? Isn't this what you wanted?"

I shook my head. "I don't want to die! I'm sorry! I won't do it again. Please don't kill me!" I begged, but the words were garbled and broken as I hiccupped between sobs.

After what felt like an eternity, Jax pulled me back, and I fell to my knees, crawling as far away from the ledge as I could before wrapping my arms around my legs. My entire body was shaking as if there was an earthquake below me, and I gasped for breath. I tried to stay as quiet as possible, biting my lower lip, but it was so hard when everything hurt.

Jax walked up to me, his haughty gaze looking down at me. He crouched down, our eyes now on the same level. The storm in his eyes had calmed, his gaze softer and gentler. He stared at me with an unreadable expression, making it impossible to know what he was plotting. I whimpered when he reached out to touch my face. "I'd miss you if you went," he murmured softly, wiping away my tears with the brim of his thumb.

"What?" I stammered.

The corners of his lip twitch, etching upwards in a sleazy smirk. "I'm saying that watching you suffer brings me immense pleasure, and having you leave would make me sad."

I swallowed thickly, trembling in front of him.

"Do you understand, Jihoon?" He leaned closer, tilting his head with raised brows. "For the first time in your life, you're actually wanted."

My chest tightened, but my heart raced uncontrollably.

"I'm the only one in this world who'll ever want someone as disgusting and pathetic as you." The sweetness he poured into his voice sent chills down my spine. His melodic voice terrified me, but I couldn't look away from his hypnotic eyes. "Do you understand?"

I bit my quivering lip but nodded.

"Good. Now wipe away those tears. I like seeing you cry, but not like this."

He gave out his hand. Hesitant at first, I took it, and he pulled me onto my feet. And just like that, with a few cruel words, Jax swayed my heart and gave me a reason to live. I was completely, utterly his.

Chapter 6: The Substitute Professor

Someone nudged my elbow, and I snapped out of my thoughts. Lola raised an arched brow, and I blinked a few times, forgetting we were still in class. Everyone around us was leaving the classroom, which meant class must have ended.

"You were daydreaming again," she pointed out, her lips slightly pulling downwards. "What were you thinking about?"

Before I could answer, she saw the look on my face and let out a tired sigh. "On second thought, don't answer that," she mumbled in a tight voice. "I might smack you on the head if you do."

I let out a sheepish chuckle before grabbing my laptop and slipping it into my bag before following her out.

"By the way, have you heard about our new substitute professor? Some of my friends saw him earlier this morning and said he's hot." She nudged me with her shoulder, giving me a lopsided grin. "Apparently, he's a total daddy."

"I'm going to barf," I grumbled, shoving my hands deep into my pocket. If there was one word I hated hearing, it was the word daddy. Jax, on the other hand... I held back a shiver. "I didn't know we had a substitute professor."

"Yeah, that's because you never listen in class. Apparently, our literature professor got into an accident and had to be hospitalized. Nobody knows for how long, but he'll probably be gone for the semester."

We walked to the next building and were about to enter the classroom, but my body froze stiff when I saw a tall man wearing a starch white shirt that was neatly tucked into his black pants. He had salt and pepper hair, an unshaven gray beard, yet a contrasting youthful face for his age, like finely aged wine. I grabbed Lola's wrist and pulled her aside.

"Ouch, Jihoon," hissed Lola, but her brows creased when she saw my face. "Are you okay? You look pale."

"That man," I whispered. "Our new substitute professor. I... I know him."

The words sent chills down my spine. She tilted her head to look at him, but I frantically pulled her back.

"Don't do that!" I hissed frantically, but she cast a skeptical glare.

"How do you know him?"

"I slept with him," I whispered weakly.

Lola's eyes widened, her jaw almost falling to the ground.

"You WHAT?!"

"His name is Will. Well, that's what I think his name is. I was too drunk to remember," I mumbled hoarsely. "I went to a random bar and got drunk."

"Without me?" she gasped in betrayal, and I narrowed my eyes. "Alright, sorry, go on."

"And he started talking to me. I thought he had a nice face and he said I looked cute. He then invited me to his house, and well, we fucked."

Lola blinked twice, stepping away from me while raising her hand so I wouldn't get closer. "Remind me never to get drunk again."

"Lola!" I cried.

She wasn't helping at all. Every muscle in my body starting to tighten and tense. My heart accelerated, my stomach heaved, and my mind buzzed in panic. Out of all the people I could have slept with, it just had to be my new substitute professor! I knew something felt odd when I saw the papers of Shakespeare on his floor, but it never crossed my mind that he could be a literature professor!

"You're going to be fine, Jihoon," said Lola, trying to reassure me. "I mean, he was drunk too, right?"

I nodded, my heart still pacing.

"Well, he probably doesn't remember you either," she said gently. "I can hardly remember the people I sleep with when I'm drunk."

I stopped, looking at her with hopeful eyes. "Really?"

"No, unfortunately, sex is actually the only thing I can remember when I sober up, but I'll cross my fingers for you."

I groaned, miserably banging my head against the wall.

"Even if he does remember, I'm sure he'll be professional about it. If anything, he'll be just as flustered as you. I mean, what's the worst thing that can happen?"

"Please don't say that," I begged, knowing that that sentence held terrible consequences.

"We have to get to class," said Lola. Before I could stop her, she already went into the classroom. I clutched my chest, taking in a deep breath before following her. I kept my head down, slightly turning my face to the side, hoping that Will wouldn't notice me. I felt like a burglar trying to sneak into someone's house.

It's okay, Jihoon, Lola's right. Will was drunk last night, so he probably doesn't remember you. Besides, if he's a professor, he's probably seen thousands of faces. There's no way he can remember all of them.

"Jihoon?"

My heart dropped to the pit of my stomach when I heard his husky voice.

Fuck, fuck, fuck, fuck... What do I do?! Do I stop walking? Do I ignore him and pretend like I'm someone else? Should I use racism to my advantage and tell him that he's probably mistaken me with another Asian? Yeah, that should work, shouldn't it?

I licked my dry lips, mechanically turning towards him with a wry smile plastered on my face. I looked into his familiar brown eyes, rimmed behind thick square glasses. "I think you have the wrong person. My name isn't—"

"Jihoon?" called Lola from her seat. "Come on, class is starting!"

Just throw me off the rooftop, why don't you?

Will raised an amused brow.

"You have the wrong person but the right name," I mumbled sheepishly.

He smiled, walking closer to me. I stepped back, accidentally bumping into the table behind me and looking like a total clutz. "It is you," he murmured, his coffee breath making me flinch. "Who knew we'd meet again like this?"

Not me, that's who.

"I didn't know you majored in literature." He smiled gently, but there was something in how he looked at me that gave me major creep vibes. And for some reason, I couldn't seem to burn the memory of seeing him lying naked from my mind, nor the image of his microscopic dick that did absolutely nothing for me.

"Your skin is so smooth and pale. Such a creamy tone, I could just bite into it." His words echoed in my mind, and I tried my best not to feel sick.

"I was quite disappointed when you left without notice," he murmured a bit quieter. I bit my lower lip but noticed his eyes lower to my neck. His Adam's apple bobbed, and I quickly stopped biting my lip.

I am not trying to seduce you, I wanted to yell at him. But considering the circumstances, I couldn't say anything. I forced another smile.

"You should start class. The other students are probably waiting for you to talk about Shakespeare or something."

But Will smiled, putting his hand on my shoulder and giving me a small squeeze. I couldn't burn my memories, but I could burn my clothes.

"My name is Mr. Gabs, but you can call me Richard outside of class." He winked, speaking low enough for only me to hear.

Just kill me now.

"I'll keep that in mind." *Creep.*

I squirmed out of his grasp and quickly joined Lola. I sunk into my chair, hiding behind my computer screen. I glared at Lola, hissing, "You threw me under the bus."

"Under the bus?" she repeated in confusion.

"I've become roadkill because of you."

"You're exaggerating, Jihoon."

"My guts are scattered across the road."

"Okay, are you done?"

I gulped and whispered, "He remembers me. He said I should call him Richard outside of class."

Lola didn't know if she should laugh or feel bad for me, resulting in a stiff chuckle followed by confused brows. "If it makes you feel any better, I prefer you date a daddy professor than that psychopathic roommate of yours," she said. "Anyone on this planet is better for you than him." A pause. "But jokes aside, if one of them tries to hurt you, I'll run over their dicks with the same bus I killed you with."

Lola always knew how to make me laugh even in the shittiest situations. Things would have been different if I had met her in high school. Life would have been better.

Mr. Gabs started class, and I leaned my cheek against my knuckles, turning my face to the side. My eyes locked with the person sitting a few tables across from me. Bus boy looked just as shocked as I did, his brown eyes widening as he recognized my face. But instead of looking away, he smiled at me, one so sweet and genuine that I blushed immediately. Without giving a smile in return, I panicked and quickly turned away. I must have looked like a complete snob. As much as I wanted to, I couldn't look at him again. My eyes wandered to Mr. Gabs, who projected his PowerPoint.

44

Right when I thought my life was complicated enough, it seemed like life wasn't planning on giving me a break.

Chapter 7: If I were Straight

It was the end of the week. I went home late because I had a project to finish with Lola and some classmates. The sun was already starting to set. I was lucky enough to find an empty seat when I climbed the bus. Leaning my elbow against the window, I stared outside, admiring the tinges of orange and red mixed with a darkening shade of purple.

While gazing at the palette of colors, my mind started to drift. I thought of how I was sexually harassed by someone on the bus a few days ago, how I had a one-night stand with my new substitute professor, how the guy who saved me from the predator was in the same class as me, and how despite all the shit I'd been through in this single day, I was still eager to go home to the person who made my life a living Hell.

"My life is a complete mess," I groaned. My phone buzzed in my pocket, and I pulled it out, unlocking the screen with a frown. It was my sister.

Yoonah*: When are you coming home?*

I typed back.

Me*: When mom and dad are willing to accept me.*

Staring at the message, I quickly deleted it and typed something else.

Me*: Mom and dad are the ones who disowned me. It's not for me to decide.*

My thumb hovered over the "send" button, but I couldn't press it. I quickly deleted everything and turned off the screen. I rarely responded to her messages and hadn't seen my sister for almost two years now. I cut ties with my family after graduating high school. My sister was the only one I kept in contact with, just to let her know that I was still alive since she was the only one in my family who cared about me—or at least pitied me.

The only home I had was with Jax.

When I got off the bus, I stopped by the convenience store to buy some food for tonight. I didn't know if Jax had eaten or if he'd be coming home tonight, but I bought two pasta boxes just in case. I placed the pre-made food in my basket but frowned. Jax was a model, and I remembered hearing him argue with his manager who had told to watch his diet.

By no means was Jax unfit. He was blessed with a wickedly quick metabolism. The guy could eat trash and still look like he had just finished a hardcore gym session. But I was worried his manager would scold him again and took out the pasta boxes, replacing them with pre-made salads with the salad sauce separated from the vegetables.

I didn't like vegetables, but Jax would probably start complaining about how I got to eat a proper meal (mind you, we're talking about industrialized pasta boxes here) while he had to eat overpriced grass that tasted like air. Aside from his psychopathic, sadistic personality, he could sometimes act like a kid. And it was cute.

I scowled at the thought. *Lola would probably beat the crap out of me if she heard me say that.*

I paid for the food and headed to our apartment, taking the elevator to the fourth floor and sliding my key into the lock.

"Jax, I'm—"

My mouth snapped shut when I saw Jax sleeping on the couch. The evening sunlight slanted gold upon his face, bringing out his nice, smooth skin. He looked like an angel, a heavenly golden boy.

I carefully took my shoes off and put on my slippers, setting the groceries and keys on the table before walking towards him quietly. I examined Jax's beautiful face as my heart pounded louder against my chest. He looked peaceful. His features were much softer, innocent almost, and his mischievous eyes were hidden behind closed lids, protected by long, dark lashes. The twisted, sardonic grin was replaced by a soft line.

A tragedy.

I reached out and gently pushed away a few strands of hair that fell over his forehead, holding my breath as I traced my fingers down the curve of his prominent jaw.

My tragedy.

In moments like these, he seemed very much human, I'd press down the painful memories and keep the tiny fragments of momentary happiness. I hated how I needed him, how much I wanted him but I couldn't. I was tied to him by a thin line that could be snipped at any moment, and it terrified me, because the one holding the scissors wasn't me, but him.

His eyes opened, and I almost gasped in surprise.

"Trying to seduce me in my sleep?" He chuckled, gently kneading his tired eyes.

And Jax the jackass was back.

"Why are you napping at this hour?"

"I was waiting for you."

I suppressed my joy with an eye roll. "Yeah, right." I snorted, heading to the kitchen. He caught my wrist and pulled me towards him, and my knee pressed against the couch between his legs to catch my balance, one hand against his chest and the other on his shoulder.

"You don't believe me?" he asked, his brows slanting up as he gazed at me.

My heart wouldn't stop racing.

"I want to," I whispered.

"Then believe me."

His right hand slipped up my shirt and roamed the surface of my skin. I bit back a moan, trying my best not to lose to him. The searingly hot and perverted hands made it hard for me to pull away.

"You're going to have to try harder if you want me to believe your lies," I mocked. I tried to get off, but Jax refused to let me go. He looked me in the eyes, and my entire body froze, almost as if he was working some kind of hypnotism with his beautiful blue eyes. His smile was replaced with an expression of worry, and his voice and touch became gentler. Softer.

"I was worried you wouldn't come back. Jihoon, I missed you."

What scared me the most was that I could no longer tell if he was still playing his games or telling the truth. Part of me wanted to believe he was horny and needed me to get it off like he always did, but the naive side of me wanted to believe him, that he actually waited for me. But my heart dropped when he tilted his head to look at me, a twisted grin pulling at the edge of his lips. "Was that believable enough?"

"Fuck you," I hissed, but he laughed, pushing me onto the couch and pinning my hands above my head. His mouth hovered above mine; his eyes half-lidded as he stared at my lips.

"I want to tie you up so you never leave my side," he whispered, his bitterly sweet words. "I want you to be mine forever. Mine only."

A sad smile pulled at my lips. "And I wish you'd die, but we can't have everything, can we?"

He blinked blankly, and with an unreadable look in his eyes, he whispered softly, "Then kill me, love."

I barely registered the heat of his lips until he pushed me to the ground, a sharp pain jolting up my back from the fall. Jax's grabbed a handful of my hair, forcing my neck back as he kissed down my collarbone. My heart accelerated and his strong thighs crushed my waist as he saddled on top of me.

"Jax," I gasped.

I bit my lip, feeling a desperate ache near my crotch. But right as things were heating up, he stopped. Jax pulled away with that domineering grin of his, gently caressing my cheek. I was about to accept his next kiss, but it never came.

"Too bad we can't do it tonight." There it was again, that wicked grin. "I'm taking my girlfriend out for dinner tonight, and I don't want any scratch marks."

He removed himself from me, leaving me speechless. *Damn it, he's messing with my head again.*

"What the hell is wrong with you?!" I demanded, sitting up in frustration.

"It's called being straight, something you'll never know," he chimed, walking past the groceries I had bought for the both of us. He didn't even glance at it and went to his room, closing the door behind him. I swore under my breath, plopping onto my back in frustration. My mind was fuming with anger, but my heart ached miserably.

The doorbell rang. Hesitant at first, I went to open the door: A beautiful, tall girl with dark hair and hazel eyes stood before me. Her ivory skin looked flawless, patted down with a thin layer of makeup. She wore a simple but elegant black dress that showed off her slim figure. She was beautiful, and anyone could tell she was a model.

"Oh, did I get the wrong address?" she asked, breaking the silence. "I'm looking for Jax."

I realized I was staring and shifted my gaze to the side. "No, you have the right house," I said in a small voice. "Jax will be out in a second."

"Are you his friend?" she asked with a polite smile, giving out her hand.

"Not exactly," I chuckled sheepishly. I was surprised by how thin her wrists and fingers were. Her body would never withstand Jax's strength. He'd break her if they slept together, bed included.

I pushed my thoughts away and shook her hand. "I'm Jihoon, his... roommate."

"He didn't tell me he had a roommate." Her words pierced me like a spear, but I smiled. "It's nice to meet you, Jihoon. I'm his girlfriend, Madison, but you can call me Maddy."

Dang it, I can't even hate her because she pronounced my name right.

She looked so kind and sweet, the type of person you wished was your friend if you had met under different circumstances. I felt guilty for harboring unjustified bitterness towards her.

"It's nice to meet you."

Jax finally came out of his room, dressed in a lovely blue shirt and his favorite pair of pants.

"Jax!" exclaimed Madison with a bright smile.

"Sorry for making you wait," he apologized, wrapping a hand around Madison's nonexistent waist and pulling her towards him and kissing her right in front of me. I looked away.

"Is that all you're wearing? You'll get cold," Jax said worriedly.

He always put on a mask, pretending to act like the nice guy in front of others when he was probably thinking of all the ways to get another woman in bed with him. He had a shitty personality but showed none of it, playing the perfect, ideal boyfriend. He was too good of a liar for anyone to find out.

"I didn't bring my jacket," she said shyly, and Jax returned with a coat and put it over her frail shoulders before kissing her again.

"Stop, your roommate is still here," I heard her giggle, teasingly hitting Jax's chest.

He shrugged. "It's fine. He doesn't care." This time she didn't resist.

"Okay, I'll go to my room now," I said flatly, knowing my existence was no longer needed.

"Hey, Jihoon?" called Jax. I turned towards him and couldn't help but frown. He and Madison looked undeniably beautiful together.

"It's called being straight, something you'll never know," his scarring words echoed in my mind.

"I won't be home tonight, so don't wait for me."

"I'm going to go crazy if I stay in this house. What am I supposed to do?"

"Do anything you like. As long as you stay close to home."

My fists tightened at my sides, my chest throbbing in pain.

"You won't go anywhere, right?"

I swallowed thickly, putting on a polite smile in front of his girlfriend. I stared at him with longing hatred, but we probably looked like normal roommates in Madison's eyes. Jax would always be the one to leave first. He left and expected me to foolishly wait for his return.

"Right," I answered, the word grating through my throat like sandpaper.

Jax 2, Jihoon 0.

Chapter 8: Kim Jihoon, a human

"Will you stop spacing out all the time?" sighed Lola as she parked her car. I turned towards her and realized I hadn't listened to what she was saying during the entire ride.

"Right, sorry," I apologized distantly, still in a daze.

"I swear, Jihoon, I'm going to slap that face of yours one day," she groaned. "And it definitely won't be because I'm jealous of your baby-butt skin, alright?"

Lola always told me how Asians had nicer skin and asked me what skincare I used. She'd get triggered whenever I told her I only used water and body lotion. Jax, on the other hand, had an entire skincare routine. *Maybe I should ask him what products he uses.* I mentally shook my head. *Wait, why am I thinking about him again? He left with Madison three days ago and still hasn't texted me. I'm sure I'm the last person on his mind right now.*

I glanced at my phone out of habit, holding on to the pinch of hope that he had sent me something. Nothing.

"H-Hey!" I cried when Lola snatched my phone away. She slipped it into her purse, out of my reach.

"We're here to have fun," she reminded me. "That means no crazy roommates. It's Friday night! Let's get wasted."

She pulled me out of the car, and we entered the bar. It was a relatively large bar, filled with loud conversations and a dominating young crowd, university students for the most part. I recognized a few faces here and there. Most of them were Lola's friends. But as we went further in, my eyes stopped on bus boy.

I spun around to hide my face. "Lola," I hissed in a low voice. "What is *he* doing here?!"

She cocked a brow. "You'll have to be a little more specific than that."

"I'll tell you who, but don't look at him."

She nodded eagerly.

"The guy at the pool table, wearing a black shirt," I whispered. But Lola didn't follow my orders and spun around, looking directly at Bus Boy. "Oh, you mean Toby?" she asked loudly, my jaw dropping to the floor.

"Lola!" I whisper-cried. "I said to be *discreet*!"

But Toby had already heard his name and approached us.

"Hey, Lola," he greeted her with a smile, his familiar tone making my heart race.

"Hiya, Toby," she beamed brightly. I stood there like a stick until Lola pushed me forward.

"This is my friend Jihoon." She leaned towards him and whispered, "He looks pretty innocent, but don't be fooled. He's really feisty with a 'tude."

I stabbed her a glare. "I'm right here, you know."

"See? Feisty," she pointed out casually. "And Jihoon, meet Toby, the guy you were checking out."

My jaw set in a hard line, heat rising to my cheeks. Toby stretched out his hand with the same eye-catching smile he had the first time I met him.

"It's nice to meet you, Jihoon," he said warmly, with a cute little accent when he pronounced my name. I wrapped my hand around his firm grip, surprised by how big and soft they felt. Toby tilted his head curiously. "Say, you look familiar. Have we perhaps met before?"

Wait, he didn't remember who I was? So the smile he gave me in class was just my imagination? Or maybe he smiled at everyone he saw. Well, it was better if he didn't remember our embarrassing first encounter. It would definitely make things less awkward.

54

"Maybe in the school halls," I said politely, slipping my hand out of his.

"Hey, Lola! Over here!" We heard a group of her friends call, and I internally panicked. My face dawned with fear, trying to beg her with my eyes not to leave me alone with Toby. But she didn't notice and said, "Toby, can you keep Jihoon company while I say hi to my friends?"

Please say no, please say no, please say no…

"Yeah, of course," he answered dutifully.

Toby didn't seem as uncomfortable as I was, probably because he didn't remember seeing an old man grind against me. The thought still sent shivers down my spine. Toby suggested we sit at the counter to order some drinks. Even sitting down, he looked tall. He had one foot on the ground while the other rested on the footrest. My legs dangled above the floor.

"So your name is Jihoon?" he asked, breaking the silence.

I took a sip of my beer to hydrate the dryness of my throat, but the alcohol only made it worse. "Yeah," I said. "It's Korean, so it's hard to pronounce. You can just call me Hoon."

"Why would I only say half your name when I can say all of it? I wouldn't like it if people called me To(e) instead of Toby."

I looked at him and couldn't help but laugh. "Right," I said, feeling myself relax. But I noticed Toby staring at me and when I raised my brows, he said, "Sorry, it's just that you look really familiar. Are you sure we haven't met? Maybe at the school dorms?"

"Oh, I don't live in school dorms. I have a small apartment not too far from the campus."

"You're lucky if you managed to find an affordable place to live. Most of my friends are drowning in student debt."

"I have a roommate who helps me pay rent. He's—" I was about to say a friend but remembered that Jax and I were far from friends. The word bully would have been more suitable, but I settled for a more neutral title. "An old classmate."

I reached for my beer and chugged down the entire cup, desperate to soothe the ache in my throat. I pulled away, coughing from drinking too fast, and Toby handed me a napkin.

"You two must be really close," he said with a smile.

That was partially true. Ironically, despite knowing him for so many years, I didn't know much about him. He rarely talked about himself. I didn't even know what his favorite color was. I ordered another beer and a shot of vodka.

"What about you? Do you have a roommate?" I asked, changing the topic.

"I live on campus. I'm actually looking for a new roommate. If you know anyone, I'd be grateful."

My brows knitted in confusion, and he read the expression on my face. "I get that look a lot," he chuckled. "Lots of people prefer having dorms to themselves, but I don't like living alone," he admitted.

"Are you an only child?"

"I have a brother, but we're on pretty bad terms," he admitted.

I usually never said anything personal, especially to someone I had just met, but maybe it was because he was willing to share something about himself that made me want to do the same. "If it makes you feel better, I'm not on great terms with my family either," I replied with a small smile. "My parents weren't happy when I told them I was going to study literature and not law."

He looked at me with an understanding nod, raising his cup. "Cheers to family."

I clinked my cup against his. "Cheers to family."

The rest of the night went by like a snap of a finger. Toby and I emptied so many cups that the bartender started to look concerned. I was good at holding my alcohol but still had limits. Conversely, Toby looked like a new client who had just arrived at the bar. I struggled to sit on my stool, and my head spun. It was getting harder for me to focus on what Toby was saying, and my eyes kept flickering towards his lips, admiring the shape of his sharp jaw before looking at the deep hues of his chestnut eyes.

I bit my lower lip as I felt his knee graze against mine, feeling a jolt of sparks. Everything felt sexual when I was drunk, which was why most of my one-night stands happened when I was completely wasted.

"Are you okay?" Toby asked, his face closer to mine than I remembered. "Maybe we should stop drinking. You look like you're burning up."

He reached over to touch my forehead, but I quickly stood up, grabbing the counter so I wouldn't fall. It would be bad if he touched me now.

"I, um, I need to go to the bathroom," I mumbled, trying not to slur my words. My legs wouldn't work properly, and it was a miracle that I made it to the bathroom without toppling onto the floor. I entered one of the stalls, locking the door behind me and leaning my back against it. My eyes swiveled towards the back of my head in a distressing sense of headache, and I arched my neck back so I wouldn't vomit. I bit my lower lip, remembering the feel of Toby's knee against mine, and mentally scolded myself for getting turned on by such a small thing.

I need to call Jax.

I searched my pockets but remembered Lola had confiscated it.

"Jihoon?" called a voice from outside. "Are you okay?"

I grumbled something inaudible. There was a gentle knock followed by a worried voice. "Jihoon, can you open the door?"

I unlocked it and opened it. "I… I need to get home."

Jax might be there.

But as I stepped forward, my leg felt numb, and I tripped. Toby quickly caught me in his strong arms, and my face squished against his rock-hard chest. The smell of alcohol was replaced by his shirt's minty pine scent, which made me feel less nauseous.

"Are you okay?" he asked frantically. I wobbled back and raised my flimsy hands.

"Don't touch me."

"I didn't. You fell."

57

Oh, right.

He didn't move, respecting my personal space. "I won't touch you," he promised. "But you're drunk. I'll take you home."

"You can't," I blurted.

"Why not?"

"Because I'm gay!" I shouted.

A deafening silence.

I waited for him to smirk and make fun of me like the students in my high school. I waited for him to look down at me with condescending eyes full of horror and repugnance like my family. I waited for him to tell me I was disgusting and worthless like Jax so often did.

"And I'm straight."

My gaze raised towards his, my brows creasing in confusion. "What?" I croaked.

He rubbed the nape of his neck with a shy smile. "Oh, I thought we were announcing our sexual orientations to each other."

I stared at him. "Doesn't it bother you that I like guys?"

"Does it bother you that I like girls?"

I scowled and said, "Of course not."

He took a step closer towards me, but I didn't back away this time. "Then I don't see why it would bother me either. Come on, I'll call a taxi for you."

Before I could protest, he bent his knees a little so I could put my arm around his shoulders. He didn't engage in any physical contact until I consented, and when I did, he held my waist so I wouldn't fall flat on my face. Nothing about his touch felt intruding or sexual. He was careful and affectionate. It was the first time someone had touched me this way. It was almost as if he was treating me as a human, as Kim Jihoon, and not a sick, gay man. And I knew that no matter how drunk I was, it was a feeling I would never forget.

Chapter 9: Jax's Pet

I woke up to a throbbing pain at the back of my head, letting out a miserable, raspy moan. My entire body felt sore, especially my throat, which still ached from chugging down so much alcohol last night. When my eyesight flittered open, I realized I was lying in bed in an unfamiliar room. Someone was sleeping on the couch across from me, but my eyes still had trouble focusing. I rubbed my eyes and blinked hard. My hand flew to my mouth. Toby was asleep, one arm over his bare torso, the other tucked behind his head. He was wearing nothing but gray sweatpants, revealing his perfectly sculpted body, which I was having a hard time not staring at.

Wait, don't tell me that we...

I looked down, and I gasped in horror. I was wearing nothing but my boxers, and my clothes were scattered on the floor beside the bed. My eyes flickered to Toby, then my body, then back to Toby, before staring at my bare chest.

No, no, no, we couldn't have. He said he was straight last night. But then why were we both half-naked?!

In a frantic panic, I ran a hand over my face and through my hair, grabbing the strands from the roots while desperately trying to backtrack on what happened last night. But all I could remember was screaming, "BECAUSE I'M GAY!" to Toby's confused face. My own voice echoed inside my mind, and I felt myself flush in embarrassment.

Out of all the things I could have remembered, my brain decided to remember *that*.

I took in a deep breath.

You need to get out of here before Toby wakes up.

I carefully got out of bed, quickly putting on my clothes as quietly as I could. I stopped at the door and looked over my shoulder. I grabbed the blanket and put it over Toby's beautiful, bare body. I didn't want him to catch a cold. He had slept on the couch so I could have the bed; it was the least I could do. Once outside his dorm room, I crouched down and clutched my chest.

"I'm so fucking stupid," I muttered, regretting touching a single cup of alcohol. My stomach hurt, and I still felt nauseous. I didn't have my phone with me, so I couldn't call anyone to pick me up. I got back on my feet, glancing at Toby's door.

Room number 1004.

***

I somehow managed to get home. I still had my wallet and just enough money to buy a bus ticket. During the entire ride, I couldn't stop groaning to myself in embarrassment, banging my head against the window while trying my best not to vomit. I was a hot mess. When I opened the door to my apartment, I didn't expect to see Jax. Yet, behold the Devil himself. He studied me carefully before drawing a conclusion that sounded more factual than a guess:

"Someone looks miserable." He leaned his strong shoulder against the doorframe, one leg crossed over the other. He wore a fancy velvet jacket and black pants, his dark blond hair neatly pushed back. He stood there, looking like America's next top model, while I looked like America's next top trash.

"You're home," I mumbled, my gaze dropping to the ground.

"I came back last night," he informed. "You would have known if you had picked up my calls."

His voice had an edge, and I knew he was in a bad mood.

"Why the hell do I have to answer your calls when you don't answer mine?" I probably didn't sound as intimidating as I had hoped. "You think you own me?"

I immediately regretted provoking him. He stood inches away, his shadow dawning over me. "You want to say that again?"

As terrified as I was, my pride refused to back down. My voice was quieter than before. "I said, do you think—"

Before I could finish my sentence, he grabbed my arm and slammed me against the wall, the door shaking from the impact. He spun me around and locked my arm behind my back, making it impossible for me to escape. He lowered his head until his lips brushed against my earlobe, my entire body freezing in terror.

"I don't *think* I own you," he growled, a smirk pulling at his lips. "I know I do."

"Let go!" I hissed. But he raised my arm higher up my back, and I let out a desperate cry of pain. "You reek of alcohol," he muttered pointedly.

"So what? Am I not allowed to drink without your permission?!" I demanded angrily.

Jax laughed, one so melodic and threatening that my body turned stiff to the bone. "Oh, sweetheart, you aren't allowed to do anything without me. What did you do besides drinking?"

I shifted my gaze to the side and refused to answer. He suddenly leaned his waist against mine, crushing my crotch harder against the wall. I grit my teeth from the pain, feeling my lower member collide against the hard surface.

"Jax, you're hurting me," I cried, but he pressed harder, and I almost screamed from the jolting pain. "I'm sorry, Jax! I won't do it again. Just please stop!"

There it was again, that haughty gaze and domineering sneer. "You'll have to do better than that, Jihoon."

My name sounded like poison in his voice. I had to choke the words out. "I'll answer your calls and texts from now on."

But he was having too much fun to stop. "And?"

"And I won't leave the house without telling you," I said in defeat.

"What else?"

I clenched my teeth, feeling like I couldn't breathe. But I forced a wry grin. "And you can go fuck yourself."

I expected him to hit me, but he grabbed my arm and pulled me to the kitchen. He opened a drawer and grabbed something silver and shiny, and my eyes stretched widely. Adrenaline pumped through my veins, and my heart raced in panic.

"Jax, wait, I'm sorry," I blurted, trying to pull away from him. "Jax! JAX!"

But he ignored my pleas and pulled me towards the living room. I tried to uncurl his fingers that dug into my skin but tripped as he yanked harder. I tripped, but that didn't stop him from dragging me across the floor. I kicked and screamed, *begging* him to let me go. He pushed me roughly against the wall, cuffing my wrist to the radiator before I could stop him. I tried to pull away, but the radiator wouldn't budge.

"What the hell?!" I cried.

He crouched down and grabbed my face, pressing his thumb and forefinger into the supple flesh of my cheeks. His crushing grip made me whimper.

"Are you going to ignore my calls again?" he asked in a terrifyingly calm tone.

It took me a few seconds to find my voice. "No," I answered obediently. I could have told him that I waited for him every day and that I didn't see his calls because Lola had my phone, but he'd twist my words and find a way to blame me.

"Don't cry, baby," he pouted, wiping away my tears. "Do you know how worried I was?" he murmured in that sickly sweet tone of his. "I thought something had happened to you. You never ignore my calls."

The hint of accusation in his tone made me feel guilty.

"I'm sorry," I mumbled, my voice shaking.

"No one will worry about you the way I do. I thought you'd know this by now."

My stomach twisted into painful knots and my burning chest started to ache.

"No one else cares about you the way I do," he continued, studying my eyes. "Do you understand, Jihoon?"

I swallowed hard, his words hurting me more than he could imagine.

No, he knew *exactly* what he was doing to me.

"You think your parents will call and ask where you are? Do you think your sister and brother give a damn about you?" he sneered, his eyes turning just as cold as the low baritone of his voice. "They wouldn't notice if you *died*."

My nails sunk into my palms, and I mentally begged myself not to burst into more tears in front of him when he brought up painful words that he knew I couldn't deny.

"Who knows? Maybe they wished you had jumped off the school building. It would have removed a huge burden from their shoulders, don't you think?"

"I'm sorry, Jax," I sobbed, tears spilling down my face. I felt embarrassed and humiliated, but most of all, *guilty*. "I'm sorry, I was wrong."

Jax wrapped his arm around me and pulled me against his chest, gently caressing my head. His warmth gave me temporary comfort. "You poor thing," he sighed quietly. "You poor, poor thing."

The warmth of his embrace vanished when he pulled away. He looked into my eyes with an unreadable expression before getting up. My eyes widened when he headed for the door. I tried to speak, but I couldn't find my voice.

He wasn't seriously going to leave me like this, was he? He wasn't going to leave me handcuffed to the radiator, was he?

Jax? Jax?! Jax!

But he left the apartment, closing the door without looking back as if he had no regret, pity, or remorse.

No, he was just upset. He was punishing me for hurting him. This was his way of showing me that he cared. It was my fault. This was all my fault. Jax didn't do anything wrong. He was innocent. My entire body shook as I stared at the quiet door, pulling my knees against my chest as I cried silently.

~~I wish Jax would come back and hug me.~~

I should have stayed with Toby.

Chapter 10: Losing my Dignity

I fell asleep against the radiator, waking up occasionally to shift my body into a more comfortable position. But after a couple of hours, my back and tailbone were sore from the stiffness of the floor. Even worse was the dryness of my throat. Thirsty, hungry, and tired, I could only wait and hope that Jax would return soon.

I sat very still, hoping someone would wake me up and tell me this was all just a bad dream. I was struck by a horrible thought: *is this what love is? Would I be trapped forever?*

I stared at nothing, lost in my own awful thoughts.

"He's fucking crazy," I grumbled miserably. When I tugged on the handcuffs, the metal tightened around my bruised wrists.

I leaned against the wall, tilting my head back to stare out the open window. For some reason, someone other than Jax popped into my mind.

Toby.

Most of what happened that night was still a haze, and my mind couldn't recollect everything, but oddly enough, a few things remained crystal clear. My left hand, the one that wasn't handcuffed, fell to my waist, on the exact area where Toby had put his when helping me out of the washroom. It was almost as if I could still feel the warmth of his fingers that seeped past the fabric of my shirt, the light scent of faded cologne tickling my nostrils.

He held onto me, and his grip was firm but gentle. The feeling was new to me. It was something I'd never felt with Jax. But a frustrated groan escaped my prickly throat when I remembered other fragments of that night. When we arrived in his dorm room, I remembered dancing and prancing around, trying to strip naked while tripping over things, before getting on my feet only to trip again.

But I was almost certain that nothing had happened between us. Firstly, he didn't seem like the type of guy to take advantage of me in that kind of situation. Secondly, my butthole didn't throb or feel sore. And thirdly, but most importantly, he was *straight*.

I hugged my knees against my chest and rested my chin on them, lips pursed. Last night was the second time he had helped me, and the second time I left without thanking him. He had shown nothing but kindness, yet I had never thanked him.

"Toby," I murmured his name under my breath just to hear the syllables. I felt the muscles near my lips pull upwards, my eyes focusing on something in the distance.

Wait, why am I smiling?

I bit my lower lip scornfully.

No, no, no, I know what you're doing, Jihoon, and no. Don't fall for someone you can't have again. He's straight. He said that loud and clear last night. Besides, he deserves to be someone much better than— My eyes stared at my cuffed, bruised wrist *— me.*

My forehead fell to my knees.

Someone like Toby deserves to be with a kind, beautiful woman who can give him things I couldn't.

But what made me even more miserable was that I wasn't talking about Toby anymore.

My ears perked up when the front door lock turned, and my back straightened immediately. Jax stepped in, his immaculate blond hair just as perfect as when he left. A golden child with a glacier heart wearing an innocent mask to hide the sadistic demon behind it. He was calm and serene, more than he had any right to be. He looked at me as if seeing his roommate on the ground, handcuffed to a radiator, was completely normal. As much as I hated seeing him, I couldn't deny that his presence relieved me. I was glad to see him and it felt so absurd I felt like laughing. He came over to me, looking down to meet my gaze. I wondered what I looked like in his eyes.

My mouth was almost too dry to speak. With a dry smile, I looked at him through my lashes. "Took you long enough."

"'Miss me?" he asked, taking off his jacket.

"As much as my parents miss me," I muttered, irony overlapping my tone. I grew anxious when he unbuttoned the edges of his sleeves, rolling them up as if he was preparing to do something.

I gulped. "Uncuff me. I need to use the bathroom."

My stomach felt bloated and pushed against my belt, my pants feeling tighter than usual around my waist. But Jax's blue eyes sparkled with evilness, and he gave me a nonchalant shrug.

"I kind of like seeing you tied up like a dog," he hummed, arms folded over his strong chest.

"Jax," I hissed impatiently, shifting on the floor to hold back the urge to pee. "I really need to go."

"Then go."

"I CAN'T!" I yelled angrily, the words ripping through my scratchy throat.

He cocked a brow. "Did you just raise your voice at me?"

My eyes narrowed, teeth grinding against one another. "No."

"And now you're lying," he mused, having fun stalling time. "You know how much I hate liars."

I scoffed with a burning glare. "Then how do you live with yourself every day?"

"I'd like to ask you the same," he bantered. I was playing a game that I was doomed to lose. He nodded towards my red wrist and pale hand. "You want me to uncuff you?"

"Yes," I answered in a heartbeat.

A sardonic grin twisted up his lips as he said, "Then suck me off."

Silence. Seized by panic, I stared at him, wondering if he had gone insane.

"What?" I stuttered in disbelief.

"If you want me to uncuff you, suck me off," he replied simply. "I've had a long day. I need to relieve some stress."

My back pressed against the wall. "You've got to be kidding me, right?"

He wouldn't do something so cruel, would he? But Jax raised his foot and pressed it against my stomach, making my eyes widen as he applied pressure. I clenched my jaw, trying not to piss my pants. He raised his brows, casting me a pitiful look.

"Does it look like I'm kidding to you?" he asked flatly. Before I could answer, he pressed harder, making me whimper.

"Jax," I choked, but he was already unbuckling his belt, his foot still pressed against me. "Jax, you have a girlfriend," I tried to reason, tears blurring my vision. "Your girlfriend, Madison, you can't cheat on her—"

His heavy black belt fell to the floor, the thud making me flinch. My body stiffened when he undid his zipper, and I pressed my hand against his ankle to stop him from coming nearer.

"Do you want to be a good little bitch and suck me off or a grown man who can't keep his own urine in his bladder?"

My teeth sunk into my lower lip; toes tightly curled as I cast him a dark glare to hide my fear. I glanced towards the bathroom. It was just a few steps away, and I had an even more desperate urge to pee. "But Madison—"

"I'll screw her later," he interrupted nonchalantly. "Right now, I want you."

Despite his cruel words, my heart fluttered. I was *wanted.*

My heart pounded with fear. He undid his pants before lowering his briefs. I took in a sharp breath when I saw Jax's cock. He was still soft, but his size was still intimidating. I swallowed hard. I couldn't seem to take him in.

"I don't want to do this," I whispered.

This was wrong. Everything about this was wrong. The fact that I'd been cuffed to a radiator for hours, that I was being pressured to give my roommate a blowjob, and that I was actually happy to hear him say he wanted me, was all terribly wrong.

Amusement glistened in his bright, blue eyes. "And since when did I give two shits about what you want?" He chuckled, slipping his fingers between my lips. My teeth were clenched tight, but he pushed them open and gained access, pressing his thumb against the surface of my tongue. He took his member with his other hand and pressed the tip against the seams of my lips. Shame and embarrassment flooded me when his cock entered my mouth. As disgusting as this made me feel, I desperately needed to empty my bladder and knew that Jax would get his way no matter how badly I protested or begged.

My mind blacked out, and by the time it ended, he and I were panting for breath. Liquid dribbled down my chin, and my entire body shook.

I wanted so badly to yell at him, to punch him in the face and swear at him. *How could someone be so cruel?* But I was scared.

Jax pulled up his pants and crouched in front of me, caressing my cheek gently. His face was so close to mine that I almost missed his smile. He cupped my face with his hands, the searing heat of his palms making me shiver.

"What, are you going to tell me that you hated it?" he asked. He grabbed my head and pushed it down, forcing me to look down. My eyes widened, blood draining down my face in horror. I quickly tried to adjust my legs to hide the bulge that tented my pants. But it was too late. He had already saw.

"*Baby*," he cooed, his voice sending chills down my spine. "You pissed your pants."

Chapter 11: Perverted Professor

As much as I didn't want to go to class the next morning, staying home was even worse. I didn't leave my room until I heard the front door close, a sign that Jax had left.

I went to the bathroom to wash my face. I had a nightmare and was still drenched in sweat. While I splashed my face with cold water, I began to cry. The tears mingled with the water, and I didn't realize I was crying until I dried my face. My hands were trembling, and my shoulders shook, and I wasn't aware I was sobbing until my knees buckled, and I crumbled to the floor. The sobs were irregular and harsh, but I couldn't feel any pain. Or perhaps I felt too much pain and couldn't point it out anymore. It was as if my emotions had been numbed, but my body still had its mechanisms.

I managed to wash up and put on an oversized sweater with sleeves that went past my wrists to hide the handcuff mark on my skin. My left wrist went from a bright red to a purplish-blue overnight. From experience, it would turn into a dull brown before healing completely. I left the apartment and took the usual bus, greeting the driver with a small smile before sitting at the back. My mind fell into deep thought.

Jax and I hadn't talked after what happened yesterday. He cleaned up my mess while I took a shower and called me to the living room when he was done. He applied some cream on my injuries, telling me we could go to the doctor if it hurt too much.

70

But what was I supposed to tell the doctor? *"Oh, my roommate handcuffed me to a radiator because I didn't answer his calls. Nothing serious."*

They'd think Jax was crazy and me even more for staying with him.

Madison came over the next day, and I had to pretend like everything was fine. It disgusted me how Jax casually flirted with her and played with her feelings, acting like he hadn't shoved his dick down my throat the other day. Madison spent the night at our place, and I had to listen to her loud moans and Jax's husky grunts, which made me feel worse for multiple reasons.

I wondered how Jax slept at night despite all the sins he had committed. Did he feel no remorse? Any guilt? Did he even have any empathy? Did he even *feel*? Despite knowing him for years, I hardly knew anything about him. He never told me about his personal life since our conversations always remained shallow. Everything was blank: his friends, his family, his childhood, his life goals. Just who was Jax Bowden?

After asking myself questions I had no answers to, I arrived at my stop. As soon as I got off the bus, someone shouted my name. Lola tackled me, and I almost fell over, bumping into a few people who grumbled in annoyance.

"Are you okay? I couldn't get ahold of you after Friday night," she gasped, touching my face and patting down my arms to ensure all my limbs were intact.

"Of course, you couldn't. You took my phone!" I snapped.

She let out a sheepish chuckle, pulling it out of her pocket and handing it to me.

"I didn't think we'd be separated. " She then glanced towards me with a curious look in her eyes. "Somebody told me that they saw you leave with Toby."

"I drank too much, and he took care of me."

A smile touched her lips, and my eyes quickly narrowed.

"No, it's not what you think."

"Did you guys do the dirty dirty?!"

"He's straight," I mumbled bitterly. "Besides, I've decided to stop sleeping with random people, especially after what happened the last time with Mr. Gabs."

Lola linked her arm around mine and pulled me closer to her as we started to walk.

"You know, Toby's a really nice guy," she began.

"Lola—"

"Even as a friend. He's a really caring guy. I think you'll like him." Her eyes twinkled before adding, "As a friend."

Lola and I made it to the classroom. I avoided Mr. Gabs' gaze, briskly walking past him and sitting at the very back with Lola. Toby entered the classroom a few minutes later, and I quickly looked away, but Lola's words echoed in my mind.

"He's a really caring guy. I think you'll like him."

Yeah, me too.

***

Class ended, and we were about to leave, but someone called my name before I could step out the door.

"Jihoon?" called Mr. Gabs, making me cringe. "Could you see me for a second?"

I wanted to tell Lola to wait for me, but she didn't hear Mr. Gabs and had already left the classroom. I bit my lower lip but turned towards him. We were the only two people in the room.

"You wanted to talk?"

"I want to touch you too," he teased. He suddenly stepped forward, putting his hand around my waist and lowering his head. My eyes shot open. This hoe was really trying to kiss me. I sprang away from him and retreated a few steps, snapping, "Sir." My heart was pounding against my chest in panic. "I think you have the wrong idea."

His brows knitted together, and I quickly cleared my voice.

"What happened between us was merely a one-night stand. Please don't think that anything is going on between us. I'm not interested in someone who's probably the same age as my dad, so I'd really appreciate it if you stopped staring at me during class. It makes me—" *want to throw myself out the window* "—uncomfortable."

"I see," he murmured, looking slightly taken aback. Mr. Gabs then chuckled. "You're more straightforward than you look, Jihoon."

I didn't know how I was supposed to take that. I simply nodded and tried to leave, but Mr. Gabs sidestepped and intruded my personal space again, asking, "How about I take you out for dinner?"

What part of "I'm not interested" did he not understand?

He grabbed my wrist, the one that was bruised, and I winced in pain.

"I can't forget about that night," he whispered, cornering me against a table. "You were perfect."

My nostrils flared. *And you were everything but perfect!*

"Mr. Gabs, please let go of me," I mumbled, trying to pull away. For a literature professor, he seemed to have a hard time understanding what I was saying. He lowered his face so close to mine that his unshaven beard scratched over my skin. "I still jerk off to your video."

My head jolted back in surprise.

"Video?" I blurted. Mr. Gabs smiled at my reaction, making me even more nervous. "What video?"

"The one I filmed," he answered.

My anxiety spiked. "What did you film?"

His smile only widened, and I already knew the answer. The blood in my face drained down my neck, making me feel dizzy and lightheaded.

"You filmed us having sex?!" I cried, unable to keep my voice steady. I was seconds away from kicking this man where the sun didn't shine, but it probably wouldn't hurt since it was so small. "Are you crazy?!"

"For you, yes."

I was speechless. Something was wrong with this man. Something very, *very* wrong.

"First of all, ew," I scowled, still trying to push him away. "Second of all, give me some goddamn space so I can BREATHE. And thirdly, delete the video!"

But he didn't do any of the above.

"Do it with me one last time and I'll delete it."

I couldn't believe this man was asking me to sleep with him after telling me he had filmed me without my consent. Was that even legal?!

"You don't want me to leak the video to the entire campus, do you?"

I swallowed hard, my fists clenching. "You wouldn't. Your face would be in it too."

But he laughed, shaking his head with a twisted grin. "It's easy to blur out someone's face."

I scoffed. "Are you blackmailing me?"

"Thursday night," he said. "Come to my place. Here's my address," he said, grabbing a piece of paper and scribbling something on it before slipping it into my pocket. Did he really think I was going to have sex with him again? And how did he expect me to trust him to delete the video?

"You expect me to trust you?!" I voiced my thoughts Why did I always end up getting involved with the most psychopathic people? Couldn't I have someone, hm, I don't know, mentally stable?!

"Look, Jihoon, I want us to be on friendly terms, maybe even more than that. I want to take care of you and treat you well. All you have to do is listen to what I say, and we won't have any problems."

A laugh escaped my lips. "Go choke on a dick."

He grinned. "I'd love to."

Mr. Gabs slid a hand inside my sweater, and his fingers made me shiver. "Just do as I say, and you'll be okay. I'll delete the footage if you come on Thursday night."

My mind was telling me to slap this bitch. If what he said was true, he could leak a sex tape of me on campus at any moment. My high school trauma of being bullied made it even hard for me to digest the potential nightmare he could cause. Would I be bullied again? Made fun of? No, I'd be too humiliated to even step foot on campus.

The memories that still haunted me flashed through my mind, and my body became paralyzed.

Faggot, chink, slut, man whore...

"Jihoon," he whispered, his finger hooking around my belt and giving it a gentle tug. "Ji—"

The door swung open and he immediately pulled away. Toby stood at the door.

"Oh, I'm sorry. Am I interrupting you two?" he asked, but there was almost an edge in his tone. He looked at me and his voice softened. "I was waiting for you, Jihoon. We were supposed to go to class together."

He was saving me.

"Right," I stammered, sliding past Mr. Gabs and hurrying to join Toby. Without turning back, I left the classroom and briskly walked down the hall. I turned around the corner and leaned against the wall, clutching my aching chest to catch my breath. Everything around me began to spin, and my chest rose and fell at an uneven pace.

Toby caught up to me and looked at me with a frown.

"You're shaking," he murmured.

"Sorry," I muttered, taking a shaky breath. "I just... I just need some space."

My knees buckled and couldn't support my weight anymore. I crouched down, feeling nauseous and dizzy.

Disgusting, disgusting, disgusting... A voice chanted in my mind.

"I'm sorry," I whispered. "I'm sor—" my voice hitched. I pressed my forehead against my knees, choking as I pleaded, "I'm sorry."

"You don't need to apologize." I couldn't see him, but I could hear his gentle voice. "You didn't do anything wrong. You're okay, Jihoon, I promise," he reassured. He gently lifted my face, wiping away my tears. Something about his touch made me feel safe.

"You'll be okay," he promised again. "I'll make sure of it."

Chapter 12: You have this look in your eyes

I took a deep breath and stood up, wiping away my tears with the back of my hands and clearing my voice so it wouldn't come out broken. I could feel my defense mechanism kicking in, making me reject any help before I became too dependent.

After taking a deep breath, I asked, "Did you hear what Mr. Gabs said?"

He nodded, and my jaw tightened.

"Can you pretend like you didn't hear anything?"

"Jihoon, this is serious. Someone is blackmailing you," he pressed with a frown. "I can't pretend like I didn't hear anything."

"Sure you can," I replied easily, almost nonchalantly. "Just squint your eyes as small as mine, and your vision will inevitably reduce. It'll almost be like you've gone blind."

Toby didn't seem to find my racist joke very funny. He stood in front of me, arms crossed over his broad chest in discontent. The image of his bare torso flashed through my mind, and I looked over his shoulder to focus on something else, hoping that the trashcan would distract me from Toby's beautiful face.

"Why do you want to help me anyway? We aren't even close," I said, deadpan. "Why were you even waiting for me in the first place? Don't you have any friends?"

I knew my voice came out harsher than I had meant, but I needed to cut things between us before it was too late.

"I wanted to talk to you after class. I didn't know what happened to you after you left my place. You disappeared without a word." He studied me carefully before asking, "Did you make it home safe?"

His sweet words and worried eyes made my heart race.

"Why do you care? We aren't friend," I snorted, trying to come off as rude as I could.

Please don't be nice to me. Please don't give me hopes and ideas that'll crush me.

He blinked, but to my dismay, he didn't seem mad or upset by my bitter words. "I like you, Jihoon," he said bluntly. My eyes widened at his words. He laughed nervously and scratched the back of his head, clarifying, "I meant as a friend. You seem really nice."

I almost felt disappointed.

"Save yourself the trouble. You won't gain anything from being friends with me," I replied dryly.

"But I already promised I'd help."

My hands tightened at my sides, and my left wrist ached. Why did I find his answer so cute? But I refused to give in. There was no way I could trust him or risk getting too close to him. Besides, he was probably offering his help because he wanted something in return. I didn't believe in free kindness. There was no way someone could be so giving. Not in this cruel world.

"Why are you so eager to help me?" I sighed, remembering all those times Jax wanted to "help" only to get something in return. My voice fell to a whisper, "Are you going to ask me to sleep with you too?"

I immediately regretted what I said. Jax would have belted me for talking back, and who knows what other twisted things he'd do. I felt my confidence shrink as the silence stretched, nervousness swimming in my stomach at the deafening silence. Toby stood still, keeping a certain distance and respecting my personal space but still standing close enough to make me nervous, but not in an intrusive way.

"You have this look in your eyes," he murmured. "You look like you want someone to reach out and help you, but don't know how to ask for it." My eyes widened at his words. His warm smile made me blush. "I made you a promise, and I want to keep it."

I made one last attempt to resist him. "You made that promise on your own accord."

"A promise is still a promise," he chuckled softly.

I gazed at him, taking in a sharp breath. Toby had eyes with a kind of beauty that expanded. His eyes were as rich as the earth's soil, like the color of hot chocolate on a cold winter night. The warmth of his gaze wrapped around me like a blanket, and I failed to resist him. I couldn't. Not with the way he was looking at me.

Chapter 13: My New "Friend"

"Okay, fine," I mumbled, pretending to be annoyed. "You can help."

Toby's smile widened, and he gave out his hand. I looked at it with furrowed brows. *Did he want to shake hands?* Confused, I shook it, but he laughed as soon as I did.

"No, silly, I want your phone. But we can keep holding hands if you want."

I reddened and quickly pulled away, stammering, "Right, you should've just said so."

I could still feel the warmth of his hand lingering on my palm. Toby started typing something into my phone, and we heard a buzz. He took out his phone.

"I sent myself a message," he explained, returning my phone. I looked at the contact's name.

Tobias Fernand.

My eyes flickered back towards Toby in curiosity. *His full name was Tobias.*

"Oh, and I almost forgot!" he said, snapping his fingers. He snapped a picture of me before I was ready. I blinked blankly, closing my mouth that hung open slightly, which only made me feel even more embarrassed.

"Did you just take a pic of me?!" I asked dumbfoundedly.

"Yeah, you look cute too," he beamed, showing me the pic. I glared at his screen. We did not have the same definition of cute.

"Delete it right now."

80

But Toby laughed, quickly dodging my hand.

"I need it for your contact pic," he protested.

"You mean that ugly picture will appear every time I call you?!" I cried.

Toby raised his brows with an ear-to-ear grin.

"You're going to call me?"

"N-No, of course not! Who would call you?!" I sneered, blushing stupidly.

Toby continued to laugh, one so carefree and musical that I couldn't stay annoyed. Toby took a selfie of himself and sent it to me. "You can save it in your phone."

I scowled. "No thanks, I don't save pictures for my contacts."

"You don't?" he asked. "I have difficulty associating people's names and faces, especially people I just met." Toby paused, looking at me with a small smile. "But for some reason, I don't have a problem remembering you."

I averted my gaze, running a nervous hand through my hair. Didn't he forget the first time we met on the bus? When I looked back at him, he still had a cheerful expression. *Who smiles so widely this early in the morning? Apparently, Tobias.*

"I guess we were destined to be friends," he said.

I pursed my lips. "We should head to class," I murmured.

Toby nodded.

"I'll text you tonight," I said. "I can't explain everything that happened between Mr. Gabs and me in person. I'd die from embarrassment."

"We'll find a solution together, don't worry."

I still had a hard time believing that someone could be so generous and kind, and I was still confused by how he wasn't disgusted after hearing I had a one-night stand with our substitute professor. But I nodded nonetheless, turning towards him with a smile. It was a small one, but genuine.

"Thank you, Tobias."

He looked surprised when I called him by his full name. Maybe he wasn't aware of it, but this was the third time he had saved me and the first time I had thanked him. I turned my face to the side, hiding the blush that worked up my cheeks. Lola was right. I was definitely going to like him.

Oh, Jihoon. When will you ever learn?

Chapter 14: A Date with a Psycho

Toby knew everything I didn't want him to know and even saw me cry. My toes clenched over the ceramic floor, warm water trailing down my bruised skin and healing injuries, and thick steam filling the air. The bathroom started to fog up, and so did my mind. The wandering thoughts and scarring memories finally quieted until I could only focus on the sound of the water sprinkling over my head.

I held my breath, tilting my head back and arching my neck to feel the water rinse my face. But my peaceful moment was shattered when I heard the front door open. Jax was home. Goosebumps ran down my arms when I opened the cupboard for a dry towel. Jax opened the door, studying my naked body from head to toe. I quickly wrapped a towel around me.

"Don't you know how to knock?!" I demanded angrily, my heart pounding against my chest.

"You look good," he noted with a hint of a smile.

"Please tell me you have a good reason for barging in here without knocking," I glowered.

His smile widened, mischief glistening in those dangerous blue hues. He asked, "Are you hungry?"

He cut me off before I could even answer. "I'm taking you out for dinner, so hurry up and change."

I took a few seconds to process what I was told. Was Jackass really asking me out right now?

"Jax, I literally just took a shower," I said, motioning towards my wet body.

I wasn't in the mood to go out with him, especially after everything what had happened. And since when did he ever take me out? We seldom did anything outside the apartment together, and I always believed it was because he was too embarrassed to be seen with me. He never took me to his school campus, never asked if he could come to mine, and refused to let me attend his fashion shows or anywhere near his workplace. I was convinced no one around him even knew of my existence.

"Besides, you hate being seen in public with me."

"Who told you that?" he asked, shamelessly staring at my nips.

I raised the towel. "Why do you want to go out and have dinner?"

"I'm taking you on a date."

He's lying, I scolded myself, but my heartbeat picked up. Knowing Jax, he was definitely up to something.

"But you never do."

"And now I am," he said smoothly. "Say yes while I'm being nice, will you, Jihoon?"

Translation: *"shut up before I make you."*

Behind his sweet smile, a devil was waiting for me to make a mistake so he could degrade and humiliate me. When he saw my hostility, he said, "I want to do something nice for you," walking towards me and raising my face so I'd look at him. I felt like I couldn't breathe, my lungs burning inside my chest. This had to be a trap.

"We'll be in a public area, so you don't have to be scared of anything happening to you," he reassured me, reading the expression on my face. I tried to resist him, but I was failing terribly.

Come on, Jihoon, you're stronger than that!

"At least you're aware of how abusive you are."

"I always have," he whispered. Was I slowly losing my mind or did he sound sorry?

"It'll be fun." The chain of words entangled me in waves of hesitation. He rested his forehead against mine, murmuring, "I want to spend time with you."

"Say, are you some kind of psychopath?" I asked bluntly, pushing him away. "No offense, but I think there's something really wrong with that head of yours."

He laughed melodically, raising his brows. "No, I just like to tease and see you cry."

Psychopath it is.

"We leave at five," he said, kissing my forehead gently before leaving. Once he closed the door behind him, I felt like vomiting. I crouched down to catch my breath. My mind was buzzing in confusion, thinking of all the possibilities that could get me into another unwanted situation tonight. My stomach twisted into a nervous knot, but my heart was pounding hard and quick inside my chest.

As absurd and ridiculous as it may sound, I couldn't help but feel happy. I hated myself for feeling this way, but Jax was giving me his attention. He wanted to go out for dinner with *me*, which he never did. Did this mean I actually meant something to him? Maybe he felt guilty for all those times he hurt me. Was Jax changing?

I looked down at my arms, saw the bruises and injuries scattered on my porcelain skin, and felt a sharp slap back to reality. I laughed hopelessly, the laughter sounding more like a terrible cry.

"This is messed up," I muttered miserably, running my hand up my face. My fingers stopped on my forehead, where Jax had left a kiss.

I got back up on my feet and dried myself, changing into the clothes I had worn earlier. My hands stopped at the doorknob, both eager and terrified to join Jax. I took a deep breath and opened the door.

Chapter 15: Mark Me as Yours

Jax drove down the busy roads, our conversations remaining shallow and aimless. Apart from sex, he never really took an interest in me, and I realized how little we spoke despite knowing each other for years. My eyes shifted towards him, looking at his side profile. It was almost as if he was a complete strange. I never knew what was on his mind. He was the most unpredictable roommate one could come across. One minute he was forcing me to give him a blowjob, and another, he was taking me out for dinner. I could never really understand him, and I wondered if anyone could.

"Are you going to stare at me the entire ride?" he mused, glancing towards me with a raised brow. I quickly looked away, hoping it was dark enough to hide the redness in my cheeks. "I don't mind. I was just asking."

His voice was not unkind, making it difficult to pinpoint his mood.

"I was looking at your window," I lied.

It felt weird sitting in Jax's car and being outside the house with him felt weirder. I was still trying to figure out what he was plotting.

Was he going to kidnap me and ask for a ransom?

My hands tightened.

Yeah, but who'd pay the ransom?

"You look anxious," he commented. "Is something wrong?"

I raked a hand through my hair, letting my palm run across the smooth strands.

"Everything, when I'm with you," I smiled sadly. "But thanks for asking."

Jax was about to say something, but my phone suddenly buzzed. I quickly turned my phone on silent before opening the message. I bit on my lower lip, fighting back a smile. Toby sent me the selfie he took earlier in the halls.

He was beautiful.

Bright, brown eyes that looked radiant even on a mobile screen, wearing a silly smile that could melt any heart into a puddle. It was the kind of photo that you wanted to keep forever. I quickly saved it and added it to his contact information.

Tobias: Make sure to save it. I'll be checking the next time we meet!!!

My mind lingered on two words.

Next time.

Toby suddenly started to call me, but I immediately hung up, glancing towards Jax, whose eyes were on the road. I let out a silent sigh of relief. I waited a few seconds before texting him.

Me: Sorry, I can't pick up right now. I'm with my roommate.

Toby: What's he like?

I bit my lower lip, thinking of the right adjectives to describe Jax, ones that didn't make him seem too... psychopathic.

Me: He's arrogant and thinks he's better than everyone else.

I sent the message and re-read it. Maybe I should say something nice to make it seem more normal. So then I wrote,

Me: He has nice hair.

My fingers tapped against my lap as I waited for an answer.

Tobias: Sounds like you like him

I scowled at the message, angrily typing,

Me: Jax can go to hell for all I care.

Tobias: Sounds like you really like him :(

I frowned. What was that frowning face supposed to mean?

Me: Stop it, To(e).

Tobias: How dare you?

A giggle almost escaped my throat, but I covered it with a small cough. I waited a few minutes before rechecking my phone.

Tobias: I know this may not be something you want to discuss, but do you have a plan for... You know.

Me: Mr. Gabs gave me his address. We have class with him tomorrow afternoon, so he'll be at school. I'm planning on sneaking into his house to find the footage.

Tobias: We'll go together.

My chest tightened as my eyes lingered on the last word. *Together.*

A voice made me jump.

"Texting your crush?" Jax asked. I raised my gaze, forgetting that he was beside me. Alarmed, I didn't know what to say. He simply shrugged. "The way you're smiling at your screen says it all."

Rather than jealous, Jax seemed calm and relaxed. Amused almost. No, he *was* amused. Why did I expect him to get jealous?

"I'm texting Lola," I said, the lie coming out as smooth as butter. "Do I have to report to you every time I text someone?"

"You're a free man, Jihoon. You can do whatever you want."

Pain wrenched inside my chest at the irony of his sentence, so out of bitterness, I decided to annoy him as well. I displayed a grin on my face, setting my jaw. "And what if I'm texting my crush?" I asked in a smug voice, just to see his reaction.

I could see the muscles in his jaw flex. "Then stop."

He almost looked upset, so I decided to see how far I could push him.

"Why should I?"

He didn't even hesitate, "Because I want your attention."

Jax wants my attention.

"I'm not going to fall for your words again."

I picked up my phone, but Jax abruptly swerved the car to the side lane. My phone dropped, and I grabbed my seat belt, my face leaning forward when Jax slammed on the brakes. I swiveled my head towards him with wide eyes. "Are you crazy?! You could have—"

He grabbed my collar and slammed his lips against mine so hard our teeth clashed. The unexpected kiss caught me off guard, getting more heated when he grabbed a fistful of my hair. He tightened his grip to arch my neck, and I winced in pain, which allowed him to slip his tongue into my mouth. I tried to push him away at first, but it didn't look like he was planning on letting me go. So I closed my eyes and went with it, letting him dominate me. His hand roamed my back, tongue twisting around mine, refusing to let me pull away for breath. My lungs burned inside my chest, desperate for oxygen. Jax bit onto my lower lip before pulling away, leaving it swollen and throbbing. He glared at me, his blue eyes looking deeper and darker than usual.

He was mad.

But a smile pulled at the corner of his lips, and my body stiffened. The deadly blue eyes that threatened to devour me glistened in the dim light.

"Don't pay attention to anyone else but me."

When I didn't answer, he released me and said, "Turn off your phone. It's ruining my mood."

I gulped, nodding stiffly. His voice was slightly off, but I couldn't pinpoint what it was. He was quiet for a moment, then finally pulled away with a sigh.

"Cross that. I'm already in a bad mood," he muttered to himself. He stepped on the peddle and drove down the main road as if nothing had happened.

My clammy hands were still tightly wrapped around the seatbelt as I faced forward. My fingers touched the throbbing area on my lower lip, but my smile vanished when I looked down. I was bleeding.

Chapter 16: Falling into his Games

We arrived at the small diner. Jax made me leave my phone in the car before getting out, but the way he "*asked*" reduced my options from two to one. I agreed without a word, not willing to risk suffering the consequences. We left his car, and he opened the door for me, and I whispered a small "thank you" before entering the building with neon letters glowing bright red above. It was a typical diner, with parents and kids, out on a family dinner to spend quality time with each other. There were also a few couples on a date here and there, but nothing special. The waiter greeted us with a polite smile and showed us to our table.

I sat across from Jax, suddenly feeling anxious again. I couldn't remember the last time we'd been together outside the house. I didn't know how he'd behave, what he'd do, or what could happen. Would he put on his mask and act like the perfectly normal roommate? Or would he do something terrible?

My eyes flickered towards a nearby couple flirting over who got the last fry. The awkward silence didn't bother Jax, but it was starting to eat me alive. I couldn't look him in the eyes, so I stared at the table, pressing my bruised lips together and hoping he'd say something instead of burning holes into me with his icy blue gaze. I didn't know if this was considered a date. If it was, it'd be my first.

Come on, Jihoon, stop getting all giddy over dinner with your roommate.

My mind paused and rephrased.

Your psychopathic roommate.

Despite mentally scolding myself for getting butterflies, I couldn't help but feel excited. Jax was like an addiction. You couldn't let him go, no matter how bad he was. The toxic pleasure of holding something unpredictable and dangerous felt good, just like how nicotine poisoned our lungs and drugs, our brains. Obtaining that short, pleasurable moment that helped us forget and cope with our real problems made us cherish it even more. Jax was my drug—even if he made me miserable, I knew I'd be worse without him.

It was even harder for me to cut him off because, unlike inanimate objects, Jax was human. He should have feelings and emotions, things he valued, and people he cared for. I always asked myself, despite his cruel and sadistic behavior, why did he save me from killing myself on the school rooftop? Why did he choose to stay with me after graduation? Why did he live with someone like me? He'd date multiple people, but in the end, he'd always return to was me. Questions like these made it harder for me to let go. It gave me hope that Jax might change, and we could become something more than simply roommates.

Hope. Yeah, that silly word led to nothing but illusions and expectations. But as much as I hated to admit it, deep down, I wanted Jax to care for me. I wanted him to become as miserably attached to me as I was to him. Me, and not some other person. Me, for who I was. Me, as Kim Jihoon. ~~Because no one has.~~

"You're staring again," he murmured in his husky voice, catching me red-handed a second time. "If you want to say something, say it."

Adrenaline coursed through my veins as I saw my reflection in his glimmering, blue eyes—cold and icy, yet so apparent.

What am I to you? I wanted to ask. I decided to change the subject.

"You're up to something, aren't you? There's no way you'd ask me to dinner if you weren't," I accused in suspicion. "Or did you bring me here because Madison couldn't come?"

The corner of his lips pulled into a lovely smile that I wanted to slap right off his face. He rested his jaw against his knuckles, tilting his head slightly as he raised his brows. "I can smell your jealousy from across the table," he mused.

"You're delusional," I replied haughtily. I inwardly high-fived myself for the sharp comeback.

"Feisty."

"Always."

Jax's lips thinned into a wider smile.

"Why are you sitting so far away?"

My hands tightened under the table, nails digging into the skin of my palms as I begged myself not to redden or look away. Lowering my eyes would be a sign of defeat, and I didn't want to lose to him. Not again. To my surprise, Jax shifted his eyes towards the window, not giving a damn about ego or pride, probably not even aware of my competitiveness. He looked outside for a few seconds, making me wonder what he was looking for. From this angle, I could see his long, dark lashes framing his ocean-blue eyes.

Why did he have to be so beautiful?

"You're suspicious."

"Of course I am," I growled. "Since when do you ask me out?"

Jax turned towards me with a different look, his smile gone.

"This is my way of apologizing for the other night. I want to make it up to you."

I sat there, staring at him in shock and confusion, a clashing mix of emotions making it hard for me to think rationally. The memories of him violently and forcefully shoving himself into me made my stomach curl and my throat burn, yet, my heart skipped at his words. The worst part was, he sounded genuine. Jax never apologized. Not once. I would have never been able to associate the word "apology" with Jax—it just wasn't something in his vocabulary.

I bit my lower lip from the conflicting thoughts that tore me apart.

~~I want to forgive him.~~ *Jax is a liar.*

"If you think buying me dinner will make me forgive you, you're wrong," I spat angrily. "What you did was— No, what you *do* is always wrong, and on so many levels that it's beyond forgiveness." My gaze bore into his. "I will never forgive you, Jax."

After a pause, he asked, "Why?"

My mouth pulled to a grimace, incredulous. "Because it's dehumanizing!" I cried, trying to keep my voice as low as I could. Anger overwhelmed me, and I couldn't hold myself back. "Don't you realize how horrible it is to humiliate someone and then make them beg? Staring at me with a grin, finding joy in making me suffer, making me *plead* at your feet while you look at me with empty eyes? Do you know how horrible that is?"

I swallowed thickly, glaring at him with so much hatred that I wished it would affect him, even if it was by the slightest bit.

"You're a heartless person, Jax, and no apology will ever change that. Truth is, you don't give a single fuck about anyone other than yourself, isn't that right?"

His answer was short. "Partially."

"Partially?" I demanded, needing more than just a one worded answer. I deserved more than that. I deserved an explanation as long as the Bible! "What do you mean, *partially*?"

Jax intertwined his fingers and rested his chin above them, leaning closer towards me. "You're sexy when you're mad. And oddly, it's turning me on. "

I swallowed hard, seeing the smirk form on his lips. Jax was normally more subtle when changing the subject. His attempt to smoothly change the subject failed, which meant that something must truly be bothering him. It was the first time I caught him off-guard. Would I finally get to learn something about him? *Keep calm, keep calm, keep calm…*

"I'm serious. What did you mean by—"

But my mouth snapped shut, and my body stiffened when I felt the tip of his foot slowly glide up my ankle from under the table. I clenched my jaw, wanting to kick his leg away. Violence was never the answer, and I couldn't find myself to hurt him, so I quickly pulled away instead.

"*Not funny*," I said through bared teeth.

"Do you remember when you were bullied in high school?" he asked out of the blue.

I blinked in utter confusion, incapable of understanding the link between playing footsie under the table and asking me about my past. But I sighed, giving up on trying to understand him.

"How can I?" I asked dully.

"Just the other day, right after you pissed yourself,"—I scowled at how blunt he was—"you came crying to my room in the middle of the night," he noted, deep in thought.

My lips pressed together. I still had nightmares about my high school days, and whenever I woke up crying, I'd always go to Jax for comfort. It was the rare few moments Jax never hurt me. He wouldn't make fun of me or berate me. He didn't even tell me to leave. Instead, he'd let me lie in bed with him, sometimes even hugging me until I stopped crying.

"Do you know why you were bullied?" he suddenly asked, snapping me out of my thoughts. "It's because you let them."

Was he really blaming me for being bullied?

"You're a coward who is too scared to stick up for yourself. You're naive and insecure, without a single backbone in your body to keep you on your feet. You let yourself be a victim because you're too scared."

I stood up, slamming my hands against the table with anger. "What the hell is wrong with you?!" I demanded, glaring into his bored eyes. "I'm sick and tired of you playing with my emotions and always blaming me for things that weren't my fault. "I knew I'd regret what I was about to say, but I was so angry I couldn't stop myself. "You know what? I'm packing my things tonight and leaving your ungrateful ass for good!"

He raised his brows. With a relaxed look, he asked, "Who else will accept you but me?"

Tears pricked my eyes. Before I could say anything, someone called his name.

"Jax? Sorry we're late. There was some traffic on the road."

My body froze to stone, immediately recognizing the voice. I didn't need to turn my head to know who it was. How could I forget such a scarring voice? But my gaze remained on Jax, whose smile only widened. This was why he had brought me here.

"Why…" my voice drifted. Jax didn't bring me here to chat or spend time with me, and it definitely wasn't to apologize. My mind yelled at me to run, but my feet felt stuck in cement.

"What do you mean, why?" he chuckled, his gaze locked on mine. "I told you I'd make it up to you."

He motioned towards the three people standing at our table, and I knew I was doomed.

Chapter 17: Old Faces

They looked just as shocked as I was, if not, even more. Jax was the only one who seemed comfortable in this situation.

"Jihoon, is that you?" asked Sam, the first to break the silence.

I gulped, turning towards him with a dark glare and clenched jaw, aware of how obviously nervous I was, yet, incapable of relaxing my tense body. My throat felt dry when I replied, "Yes."

Sam, Layla, and Kevin, my old school bullies, stood there, wide-eyed and confused. Even though it had been years since I'd seen them, I could never forget their faces. How could I forget the people who tormented me for so long? After graduation, they probably forgot about me and erased my existence from their mind, but I was scarred for life. Anxious, I clenched and unclenched my fists under the table.

"I thought it'd be nice to have a small get-together," Jax said, filling the awkward silence with his smooth tone. He turned towards me with a curve on his lips. "You don't mind if our old friends join us for dinner, do you?"

Applying the word "friend" to these people was like pressing alcohol against an open wound.

"It does bother me," I answered firmly. "In fact, having dinner with you bothers me too."

How stupid could I be? To believe that Jax had a heart, or at least enough empathy to feel bad for the terrible things he had done to me, was incredibly stupid.

"I'm leaving."

I stood up when Jax asked, "Where do you think you're going?"

"Away from you."

"I'm your ride home."

"I'll call a taxi."

"Your phone is in my car."

I gritted my teeth. "Then I'll walk home."

"You don't know the way back, and even if you did, it's too far." I stared at him, wondering how deeply he had plotted this night. Sam, Layla, and Kevin's eyes flickered back and forth as if they were watching a ping-pong match I was losing.

"You're ruining the mood," sighed Jax, running a hand through his gold hair, his pretty blue eyes so full of evil to a level past my comprehension. I bet if you stared long enough, you'd drown. "Stay."

Despite his sweet tone, there was something dangerous lingering in his gaze. What did he expect me to do? Pretend this entire situation didn't bother me, throw my head back and cover my mouth, shaking with laughter at jokes made by people I never wanted to see again? *Oh, Jax, you are hilarious.*

He didn't wait for me to answer and turned to his friends. "You should sit. It's been a while."

To my horror, the three of them did. Layla turned towards Jax, batting her long lashes coated in thick mascara that looked like tarantula legs. "I didn't think you could get any hotter, Jax." She said his name as if he were a god, and I struggled not to gag.

"May I take your order?" asked the waitress in a perky voice, mainly looking at Jax. She'd been glancing at ever since we stepped in.

"Order whatever you want. It's on me," Jax said nonchalantly.

My brow furrowed in confusion. Was he really willing to pay for them? I knew he was earning money through his modeling gigs, but it still seemed a lot, especially for people he didn't consider as his friends but mere pawns to play with when he had nothing to do.

"You don't have to," I mumbled. I wasn't trying to be polite, but I didn't want Jax to pay for them or for me. He shouldn't. But the others didn't seem to mind.

"Really? That's so sweet," awed Layla with a fake giggle as she wrapped her arm around Jax's, earning a frown from the waitress, who impatiently tapped her pen against her pocket-size notepad.

"You sure?" asked Sam, pretending to look bothered when his eyes were already on the menu. Out of all the jerks that could have sat down beside me, it had to be him? I would have preferred Kevin. He had done the least damage among the three, only having stolen my lunch money. I felt uncomfortable when Sam's large shoulders brushed against mine, and my eyes darted to Jax, hoping he'd save me.

"Like I said, it's my treat," said Jax smoothly. "That goes for you too, Jihoon."

Before I could protest, the others were already ordering their food, choosing the most expensive dishes their broken asses probably couldn't even afford. It was my turn, and I looked at the menu, avoiding the food that cost over twenty dollars, and went for a small house burger and fries.

"That's the kids' meal," the waitress said, and I stiffened. I was so fixated on the prices that I didn't notice.

"I don't eat a lot," I murmured, feeling my face redden slightly. Everyone at the table stared at me.

"Are you sure?"

I nodded, dropping my gaze.

"No desert?" she asked. Everyone else had ordered one.

"No, thank you," I said, handing her the menu.

"He'll have a strawberry milkshake," Jax said.

I bit my lower lip. "I don't want a strawberry milkshake."

"You love strawberries."

"Yes, but—"

"And milk."

I hesitated. "I do..."

"If you can't finish it, we'll share." Before I could protest, the waitress already focused her attention on Jax, asking in a brighter tone, "And what would you like?"

"I'll take a chicken salad." He patted the area of his shirt that hid a perfect six-pack. "I'm trying to watch my weight."

"Oh, you really don't need to," she giggled, tucking a lock of hair behind her ear.

"Manager's orders," he sighed with a smile.

When she left, Sam leaned forward. "Jeez Jax, you're still just as popular with the ladies as you were in high school," he mumbled, envious. "And you got even taller and handsome. What's up with that?"

"He's Jax Bowden. What did you expect?" swooned Layla, still clinging to someone who wasn't hers. I wanted to tell her that Jax had a girlfriend in respect for Madison, but she probably already knew that. Jax was always with a girl. He had the "can't-be-single" syndrome, but that didn't stop women from wanting him.

"I saw you in a fashion magazine. Is it true that you model now?" she asked.

"Only part-time," he nodded humbly.

Layla looked impressed, while the two other boys looked jealous. They continued to talk despite the implicit rivalry. Jax never had a problem getting along with people. He was confident and outgoing, knew what to say and do in the right moments, and had the gift of naturally attracting people around him.

"What about you, Jihoon?" Sam smirked, glancing down at me. "You look like you've gotten skinnier. You should put some more meat on those bones."

He squeezed my arm, and I jumped slightly when his grip crushed my bones. A thousand memories flashed through my mind when he touched me, the countless beatings and injuries he had given me. I opened my mouth to say something, but nothing came out. I stared at my lap, hoping he'd let go.

"Touch him again and I'll break your wrists."

Jax smiled, his voice calm but strong. It was the type of tone that sent chills down your spine. There was a dangerous fire burning in his blue eyes. Sam got the message and immediately released me.

"I was just kidding," he chuckled, but I could tell he was slightly shaken by the warning.

"So, how did you two get together? I thought you cut ties after high school," Kevin said, staring at me. "You two weren't that close back then."

I could read the look in their eyes. *Why are you with someone who made your life a living hell?*

I didn't answer, wondering what Jax would say. Would he be too embarrassed to admit that we were roommates and shrug it off with a lie? Plausible.

Chapter 18: His Apology

"We're roommates," Jax replied. "We moved in together after graduation."

Layla jerked her head back and almost obnoxiously asked, "Wow, just like that?" Her eyes flickered from me to Jax before biting her lip coated in ruby red. "Say, are you two perhaps…"

The three of them eagerly looked at us with toxic curiosity.

"Come on, Layla, are you implying that I'm a fag?" Jax snorted and my heart crushed within a few seconds. Layla's brows furrowed at the last word. "Why do you look so surprised? You guys used to always call him that."

His grin widened, revealing his pearly white teeth.

"You're not going to act like we didn't bully him, are you?" He laughed with almost an edge to his voice. "Jihoon doesn't care. It's all in the past. No hard feelings."

Jax's words were almost an encouragement, and Layla was the first to speak up, the look in her green eyes turning vicious.

"Don't you get scared sometimes?" I thought she was talking to me until I realized she was facing Jax. "I'm not sure if this is entirely true, but I heard that liking the same gender can be contagious." She cast me a nasty look. "No offense, John."

"Jihoon," I mumbled.

"Can you even relax at home? I'd be nervous if I were you," Sam said before adding, "No offense," as if that would make it all better. "I wonder how gay guys even— You know," said Sam, waving his hand as he teamed up with Layla. "Like, where does it go? They only have one hole, and it's pretty disgusting if you think about it." Another glance. "Again, no offense Jihoon. I'm, like, totally not against the ABCD community."

Layla bit her lip to hold back her laugh.

"It's LGBTQIA+," I grumbled under my breath, but I guess it was too many letters for his small brain.

I noticed that I was clenching my fists so tightly on my lap that they were trembling. Forgetting the past wasn't easy, especially when they left such deep scars that still gave me nightmares. I could feel their eyes drilling holes, staring at me with faces that masked a dirty sneer. I should have never followed Jax here. Why in the world did I think we'd have a nice time out?

~~Toby Toby Toby Toby.~~ *Maybe I can ask Lola to pick me up. Yeah, but my phone is in his car.*

"Have you never tried anal?" asked Jax. Kevin spit out the water and quickly apologized. Jax had a smug smile, raising his brows with a condescending gaze.

"You must have really boring sex." A shrug. "I get it. You prefer vanilla." Sam's jaw ticked at his words. "Or maybe you're still a virgin."

Sam's face burned bright red from his neck to his hairline, both embarrassed and angry, but Jax didn't care.

"So, what are you three studying? Are you doing anything interesting with your lives?" he asked casually, pouring himself a cup of water and taking a sip. No one but Jax could make drinking water look classy, obnoxious, and sexy all at once.

"Economics, but I'm thinking of changing majors," said Layla, the first to answer. "Kevin is taking a year off, and Sam is re-doing his first year."

"So basically nothing interesting," said Jax. They flinched at his words. "Then again, you didn't learn much in high school. All you did was copy off of Jihoon and cheat on your tests. I guess karma caught up to you."

Layla's grip slowly loosened around Jax while Sam narrowed his eyes. "You did the same," he snarled. "You're no better than us."

"Oh, I'm way worse," he chuckled darkly. "But the difference between you and me is that I'm not a broke virgin who is still living under his parents' roof."

Sam's mouth dropped in shock, and my eyes widened. What was Jax doing? He was normally the one bullying me, not the one taking my side. I shouldn't be enjoying this so much.

The feeling of having Jax by my side felt empowering. It made me feel invincible. Jax's phone suddenly buzzed, and he looked at the screen.

"I'll have to leave our little reunion early. My girlfriend is calling."

"What about the food?" Sam frowned.

Jax stood up, saying, "Enjoy the meal. Like I said, the bill is on me." Jax smiled, putting a hand on Kevin's shoulder, who flinched under his grip.

"Don't look so uncomfortable. The three of you always loved leeching off other people's money. Right, Jihoon?"

I was too stunned to speak.

The tension in the air intensified, but their anger couldn't match Jax's confidence. Layla looked like she was both hurt and turned on, while Kevin seemed confused and guilty. Sam looked furious. I sat there, not knowing what to do or say. Jax never took my side before, not like this, and I didn't know how to react.

Jax was about to leave but stopped. He looked over his shoulder, his gaze locking on mine.

"Aren't you coming?"

My back straightened, and I quickly slid out of the booth, glancing at my old school bullies one last time. They looked pitiful. And that was the greatest revenge I could ever get. I followed Jax out of the restaurant. We got in his car, and he drove out of the parking lot. I kept fidgeting, eyes indecisive on where to look at.

"Why did you do that?" I finally asked.

"I told you I'd apologize."

I bit my lower lip.

"You've been having nightmares about high school lately, haven't you?" Before I could deny it, he said, "You talk in your sleep."

Was that why Jax planned this whole dinner? To get back at my bullies for me? But why?

"Jihoon," he said, eyes still on the road. "If you think I'm capable of emotions like love or empathy, you're sorely mistaken."

My chest tightened when he looked at me.

"But for some reason," he murmured, his eyes lowering to my lips before settling on my eyes again. "You bother me."

My emotions were jumbled up, pixels of memories from the past flashing through my mind. The nauseous feeling in my stomach worsened, and my entire body shook.

"Jax," I murmured weakly. "Jax, stop the car."

He didn't answer.

"Jax," I begged, feeling sick. "The car."

My stomach lurched.

"Jax—"

He stopped the car around a curb. I quickly opened the door, stumbling out and falling to my knees. I crawled forward before vomiting. I expelled everything, coughing and gagging as I grasped the grass beneath my palms. Sweat trickled down the goosebumps on my skin. I wiped the saliva dribbling down my lip with the back of my hand, panting heavily. My entire body felt cold, as if the temperature around me lowered drastically within seconds.

Footsteps came forth, and I turned my head, looking up at Jax. I squinted, the bright headlights almost blinding me. Jax appeared like a dark shadow until he crouched down to my eye level, unbothered by the vomit in front of me. He didn't ask if I was okay. He didn't offer kind words or affection. Why? He was Jax. Simple as that.

His face was close to mine as he looked into my eyes with an unreadable expression. Jax would remain a dark shadow that cast over my life forever. He was destructive and toxic, yet, I couldn't hate him.

He couldn't say sorry, but he showed a glimpse of empathy in his own twisted way. He reached out and brushed away a tear. My heart fluttered when he gave his hand and whispered, "Let's go home, Jihoon."

Even if everything was calculated and prepared, only Jax could give me such an absolute and satisfying revenge.

~~*I forgive him.*~~ *What a manipulative bastard.*

Chapter 19: A Glimpse of Freedom

I heard my alarm go off and opened my eyes. I'd usually feel hazy when I first woke up, but it was almost as if I hadn't slept at all. Something tightened around my waist. I turned to the side, taking a sharp breath when I saw Jax's face only inches away from mine. He was shirtless, just like every morning. He always hated sleeping with clothes on. Jax looked so different when he was asleep. He had the same face and features: high cheekbones, nicely accentuated face, flawless skin… But so much less harmful.

Is this what he looked like when he was a kid? I wondered.

I wanted to ask him so many questions and understand how he became so complex.

"If you think I'm capable of menial emotions like love or empathy, you're sorely mistaken."

My lips pressed together.

"But for some reason, you bother me."

Was Jax really as cruel and heartless as he acted? Or was it a character that he molded for himself? I couldn't understand him. I reached out and touched his face, staring at him in confusion and frustration.

Why can't I understand you?

Jax opened his eyes, startling me. I quickly pulled my hand away, but he took my hand and placed it against his chest. I could feel his heartbeat against my palm. *Maybe he is human, after all.*

"I have to go. I have class."

"Call in sick," he replied huskily. I could tell that he was annoyed. It was cute.

"Do you really expect me to spend the rest of the day in bed with you?"

"Yes."

"Stop acting like a spoiled brat," I muttered. "You have to work this afternoon. Your manager's going to get mad again if you don't go. I bet you would have been fired a long time ago if you weren't so popular in the industry."

"You're so stupid," he murmured.

I snapped him a glare and scoffed. "Excuse me?"

His fingers wrapped around mine when he said, "Even in moments like these, you put me first. You always put others before yourself, even when the world has done nothing but make you miserable. It's sad."

"If you feel so bad for me, why don't you try being a little nicer? Oh, right. You don't feel anything, do you?"

He displayed his perfect little smile. "You have me all figured out."

"One day, I'll leave you," I murmured, pulling myself towards the edge of the bed. My body stiffened as my bare toes touched the cold floor. "And you'll regret everything."

I didn't think he heard me until he said:

"I probably will."

My eyes widened, turning towards him in surprise. Jax lay there, one hand tangled in his messy bed hair, staring at the ceiling with an expression I couldn't quite read. His blue orbs then flickered towards me, and the edge of his lips hiked up. "Sike."

My jaw clenched, mentally groaning for believing him again. "You're such a dick," I hissed, throwing my pillow at him.

He caught and hugged it instead, resting his chin on the soft surface. "Hey, Jihoon? Who do you hate the most in the world? Your parents, your bullies, or me?"

"Do you really need to ask?"

107

He reached out, his index finger curling around mine. There was a short pause.

"Don't hate me."

My brows pulled together. "What?"

He smiled, but there was nothing arrogant about it. "What if we tried starting over again?"

I blinked at him blankly. *Start over? Did he expect me to forget everything he had put me through?*

"I need some time away from you before I can even look at you without wanting to punch you."

"If distance is what you need, I'll give it to you."

Repairing the damage would take much more than distance, I thought to myself. But his questions confused me. Was he scheming something again? Plotting another cruel trap before humiliating me?

He leaned over and grabbed something from the drawer where he kept our sex toys. I didn't like where this was going and attempted to get up and leave, but he pulled me back, sitting me between his legs. I frowned, trying to squirm away, but he pressed my back against his chest and rested his chin on my shoulder.

"Open your legs."

My eyes stretched at his request, knees turning inwards.

Jax pried them apart. "It won't hurt," he promised.

"J-Jax," I stammered, blushing furiously. He removed my pants, and even though I was wearing his shirt that was big enough to drape over my waist, Jax raised the hem of my shirt. His gaze fell on my semi-hard member.

"Does this turn you on?" He chuckled, and I reddened.

"It's your hands," I blamed.

He grinned and whispered, "Shameless," into my ear as he traced his hand down my abdomen and closer to my lower part. *"You want me."*

I held back a whimper as his hand went further down. He kissed me roughly, and I could feel everything, my cock twitching when his tongue pressed against mine. Jax smelled good. He always did. I held him tighter, wanting his smell to rub off on me. Jax was an amazing but rough kisser, often leaving my lips sore and craving more. Even when he nibbled or bit my lip, sometimes even choking me a little too rough, something about his touch drew me in. His kisses were deep and sexual, making my mind numb. No matter what he did, I couldn't turn him down. He was attractive and horrifying all at once. On rare occasions, he could be lovely. Jax ran his hand through my hair and gave it a tug, making me wince. He pulled away and replaced his mouth with a cold object. He coated the vibrator with my saliva before taking it out and inserting it elsewhere. I almost yelped when I felt the tip of the toy poke at my hole.

"Jax," I gasped, feeling him push it in. I couldn't help but moan, my back arching against him as I gripped his arm. I bit my lower lip as he pushed further into me, but my eyes opened when he pulled my pants up.

"Aren't you going to take it out?" I demanded.

"No."

"Jax, I have class!"

"Then keep it in during class." He shrugged nonchalantly, wrapping his arms around me and hugging me affectionately. "If you keep it in until I return, I'll reward you."

"I don't need your damn reward! Screw this. I'm taking it out."

I shoved my hand angrily inside my briefs but froze when he whispered softly, "I'll grant you a wish."

I met his eyes, the mysterious and unpredictable gaze making me anxious. He took my hand and intertwined his fingers with mine. "If you keep it in until I come back, I'll do anything you say," he promised, his chin still on my shoulder as he lifted our hands to the light above us. "I'll even kill myself."

"You're out of your mind." I laughed, staring at him in disbelief. He placed his palms on the bed and leaned back, giving me another one of his infamous smirks, but this one looked almost wistful.

"You always wanted me dead, haven't you? Or maybe you've changed your mind."

I was speechless. What terrified me even more was that I didn't know if he was joking. How could he speak so lightly of something so serious? He tilted his head, asking, "No wish?"

"Screw you," I snarled, glaring at him. "If I keep this damn thing inside me until you get back, I never want to see you again."

He raised his brows with a whistle.

"That's a mighty wish you've got there. Do you think you can live without me?"

"Absolutely."

My anger drove an immediate response, but that instant reply sparked regret. Thoughts dashed through my mind, but before I could take back my words, he said, "Alright." His answer was slow and showed no emotions that indicated his true feelings.

"If you win, I'll let you go. But if I win, you'll be mine forever."

I knew Jax was up to something. He always was. But I didn't bother trying to figure him out this time. I held his gaze, and with fake confidence, I declared, "Deal."

Chapter 20: Crook with a Boner

I felt like everyone on the bus was staring at me when they probably didn't give a damn. They were all too busy staring at their screens or were drowned in their music. I held onto the handle, squirming and shifting as I tried to stand comfortably, but how could I when there was a CUCUMBER-SHAPED OBJECT VIBRATING INSIDE OF ME?! The bus went over a bump, and I bit my lower lip as the demonic thing shifted, hitting me in the right spot. I tightened my grip, taking a few deep breaths to calm myself down. *It's going to be okay. All you have to do is—*

My spine jolted straight. "Fuck," I rasped when the bus hit another bump. A little girl who stood beside me raised her head with furrowed brows, and I let out a nervous chuckle. "I, um, I didn't mean to say—"

"Fuck you too, sir," she said, walking to the back of the bus, as far away from me as possible. I blinked in shock and confusion. *Alrighty, then.*

After thirty minutes of torture, I finally made it to my stop. When I got off, Toby was sitting on a wooden bench waiting for me, greeting me with a heartwarming smile. He was wearing a dark green sweater, a pair of black jeans, and an expensive pair of sneakers. His chestnut eyes were framed behind glasses, making him even hotter than he already was. Toby ran a hand through his lustrous hair, and I was so mesmerized by his radiating beauty that I forgot to breathe.

"Hi." I almost stuttered when he stood up, his tall height dawning over me. "Did you wait long?"

"No, I arrived a couple of minutes ago. Are you ready to break in and commit a crime?"

I scowled. "Aren't you being too enthusiastic for someone who's about to break the law?"

Toby let out a small chuckle, raising his glasses up the bridge of his nose. I always found it irresistibly hot when guys did that.

He's straight, Jihoon, remember that.

He shrugged and said, "I'm excited to help you."

I had to repeat the sentence over and over in my head. *He's straight, he's straight, he's straight, he's straight... ~~Fuck, he's hot.~~*

I quickly looked away and pulled out the crumpled paper Mr. Gabs slipped into my pocket the other day. "This is the address he gave me."

Toby nodded, typing the location into his phone. "He only lives fifteen minutes away from here. We should hurry up before Mr. Gabs' lecture ends."

I nodded and followed Toby; my eyes focused on the ground while I tried to ignore the vibrations that made me sensitive. This wasn't the ideal situation to be in. My mind suddenly flashed to the image of Toby's shirtless body, and I mentally shook my head, scolding myself for having dirty thoughts when he was right beside me.

This isn't the time to be horny!

"Do you mind if I ask you something?" Toby asked.

"Mhm."

"Why did you sleep with Mr. Gabs?"

~~I was tired of waiting for Jax.~~

~~I needed a distraction.~~

~~I wanted to make my roommate jealous.~~

"I was bored," I replied. "I wanted something casual."

"Wanted or needed?"

I flinched.

"I just don't think I'm ready for a relationship."

"Oh."

I glanced at him. Why did he sound so glum? Did I upset him? Or maybe he was too disgusted by the fact that I had slept with a random man much older than me.

"I get what you mean," he said, exterminating all the negative thoughts with his calm, smooth voice. "Relationships can be complicated, and emotions are messy." A pause. "I was in one a few months ago."

"You're single?" I blurted so bluntly that I felt embarrassed. *Shit, I shouldn't sound so happy.*

He laughed with a nod. "Yeah."

"Well, you know what they say. There are plenty of frogs in the sea."

Toby stared at me with a strange grin.

"You mean fish?" he asked gently.

"What fish?"

"There are plenty of fish in the sea," he rephrased.

"Uh, no, I'm pretty sure it's frogs."

Toby smiled, then shrugged, casually saying, "Frogs can work too." He leaned over and tousled my hair, his touch sending sparks from my head down to my toes. I felt like the vibrator intensified the second we were in contact, and I jerked away, trying to keep my breath steady while walking in the least awkward way possible.

"Sorry, I don't like it when people touch my hair," I lied. I couldn't have said an even worse lie. I loved it when people I liked touched my hair.

He nodded but didn't apologize, almost as if he knew I was lying. I secretly hoped he did. We continued to talk on our way to the address.

"It should be this one," said Toby, stopping in front of the house with Mr. Gabs' name written on the mailbox. The house was big, with at least two floors inside. There were creepy gnomes staring at us from the front yard. I held back a shudder. We walked up to the porch, but the door was locked.

"We can try going through there," suggested Toby, pointing at the open window on the second floor.

I frowned. "We don't have a ladder."

"You can climb on top of me."

I never thought I'd hear a straight man say that to me. Before I could protest, Toby stood under the window. He cupped his hands together and bent his knees slightly.

"You can step on me," he said, and I scolded myself for having such a dirty mind. "And I'll hoist you up."

"I don't know if I can."

"Of course you can," he said, eyes bright and fully confident. "I promise I won't drop you."

Toby had more faith in me than I did in myself. I bit my lower lip, looking up towards the window before looking back at Toby.

"Promise?"

"Promise," he nodded. I slowly started taking my shoes off, stiffening when the object inside shifted inside me again.

"You don't mind touching my socks?" I asked. "I-I promise they're clean—"

"It's fine, Jihoon," he chuckled.

I forced a nod, putting one hand on his strong shoulder. He hoisted me up, but I felt the toy shift and pulse against an area I didn't want it to be pulsing against, and I almost groaned. My feet landed on the ground again.

"Are you okay?" Toby asked worriedly.

I forced a *mhm*, and we tried again. He hoisted me up, and my knees buckled as the vibrator hummed against all the sinfully right places. I got back down and let out an annoyed groan, begging my body to control itself.

"Jihoon," murmured Toby, his voice sounding like sex to my ears. *Why, oh why, was this happening to me?!* "If you're scared..."

"I can do it," I pressed in a strained voice. "I can do it, just give me a sec."

114

I was trying to break into my professor's house to steal an illegal sex tape when I had a vibrating sex toy shoved deep inside me while standing in front of my straight classmate who looked like a gift from the gods. I took a deep breath to calm myself, begging my body not to get an erection.

"Let's try again," I winced.

Toby studied my face and looked hesitant, but I climbed on top of him, and he pushed me up, clutching onto the window ledge for my dear life. I managed to pull myself up and wiggled through the window, crashing gracefully to the floor. I let out another groan, rubbing my sore elbows.

"Are you okay?" Toby shouted.

I'm trying not to have an erection.

"Amazing," I replied grimly. "I'll open the front door for you."

But when I got up, I saw myself in the mirror and took a sharp breath when I saw the lump in my pants.

I was hard.

Chapter 21: Arousal

I started to panic, but this was not the time or place to jerk off. The best I could do was pull down my sweater and put on a straight face. *Ha... Straight.* I scurried downstairs and opened the door for Toby.

"This place is huge," Toby murmured in awe. I was so busy panicking about my boner that I didn't notice how big the house was. Toby looked at the pictures hanging on the wall and frowned. In the frame, Mr. Gabs was wearing a tuxedo beside a beautiful woman in a wedding dress. An expression of disgust and pity crossed his face when he stepped towards it.

"He's married," he said before turning to me. "Did you know?"

"No, I didn't," I murmured, feeling my stomach twist into a knot. The fact that I had slept with a man who was married to someone he swore to protect and love for the rest of his life made me feel sick, but at this point, I wasn't surprised by how low I could stoop. Even if it was unintentional.

Toby's eyes studied my face, but I couldn't meet his gaze. "It's fine, Jihoon. You didn't know."

"You don't need to make up excuses for me," I whispered, walking up the stairs, but Toby caught my wrist. An electric sensation shot up my arm when his skin touched mine, almost making me whimper. His hand felt warm, and I wanted him to tighten his grip. I was horny as hell, and I didn't know what to do.

"Jihoon," he said firmly, making my knees buckle. The vibrator continued to pulse inside my walls, and I was having a hard time keeping my breath steady. "You shouldn't be so hard on yourself all the time."

The way he looked at me made my heart throb.

He's straight, he's straight, he's straight!

"Let go," my voice hardly a whisper. I bit my lower lip, trying to keep calm.

He studied my face. "Is something wrong?"

What's wrong, is that I want you to pin me against the wall and kiss me. What's wrong, is that I find you utterly attractive even though you're straight. What's wrong, is that I have a vibrator inside me and I want you to use it to play with me. What's wrong, is that I'm gay, and I'm seriously falling for you!

"You're red," he murmured, placing his hand against my forehead to check if I had a fever. My eyes flung open as a tingling sensation shot down my spine just by the touch of his hand against my face. I could feel my erection throbbing against my briefs, desperate to be touched and played with. Toby was too close, and I was too vulnerable. This was messed up.

"Do you think you can live without me?" Jax's voice echoed inside my panicking mind.

The vibrator hit my prostate, and I gasped, my knees so weak that I had to hold onto the handrail for support.

"Jihoon," he began, but I cut him off.

"Don't."

"Why are you always pushing me away?"

The vibrator continued to tease my prostate, and I covered my mouth to stop myself from making any noises. My eyes fell to Toby's lips, and I was tempted to kiss him. My desires were taking over my rationality, and Toby reached out to touch my face.

"Jihoon?"

But it was as if I couldn't hear him. All I could focus on were his lips. I was desperate and losing control. I made a decision I knew I'd regret, grabbing him by the collar and pulling him in.

Before his lips could touch mine, we heard keys jingling from outside. Toby and I exchanged a frantic look. He grabbed my hand

and pulled me upstairs, running into the first room in the hallway. We hid inside a closet, hearing the front door open. The closet was stuffy, giving us absolutely no space whatsoever.

"Mr. Gabs shouldn't be here. He still has class," whispered Toby, his breath dancing against the nape of my. My teeth sunk into my lower lip to muffle back a whimper, feeling my briefs tighten to the point where it hurt. I could feel Toby's broad chest against my back.

Fuck me.

"It could be his wife," I whispered back, trying to create some distance between him and me, which obviously didn't work. I took a shaky breath, my body tingling from the vibrator. I couldn't take it anymore.

"Toby," I whimpered, digging my nails into my clammy palms.

"Yes, I'm here."

Oh god, his lips were inches away from my earlobe.

I had difficulty standing properly, my eyes rolling to the back of their sockets. At this point, I was panting heavily, starting to reach the orgasm I'd been holding back since Jax put the cursed thing inside me.

"Are you sure you can live without me?"

"Toby, there's something inside of me. You have to take it out," I begged weakly, squirming around. I'd suffer the consequences of unimaginable embarrassment later, but I couldn't hold it in.

"In… Inside of you?"

We heard footsteps making the floor creak. There was a female voice and a male voice, followed by giggles. I nodded quickly, turning my head around to look at his face. But it was too dark for me to see anything.

"My pants. There's something inside my—"

We heard the door open, the sound of laughter intensifying. I peeked through the small crack and saw Mr. Gabs' wife step inside with another man. She pushed him onto the large bed, removing his shirt and throwing it aside. My mouth dropped wide open in shock as he pulled her down with him, pinning Mrs. Gabs against the sheets, devouring her in kisses while she wrapped her legs around his torso.

"Don't leave any marks," she gasped in half a moan. "He can't know about us."

Only someone who didn't want to get caught would say something like that. I would know. Was she cheating on Mr. Gabs?

"Fuck, you're so sexy when you moan," growled the man, skimming his hand up Mrs. Gabs' skirt. "Mmmh, good girl."

He stuck his head up Mrs. Gabs' blouse, pulling up her bra and sucking her tits, making Mrs. Gabs scream and laugh simultaneously. Watching them make out was beyond awkward. I came here to find my sex tape, not watch someone else have sex!

I didn't know what was worse, witnessing Mrs. Gabs be called a good girl while having her nips sucked dry or almost having an orgasm in front of Toby.

I was biting so hard on my lower lip that I was persuaded I was bleeding. I felt Toby move behind me, but I couldn't tell what he was doing. A gasp escaped my throat when the toy continued to hit near my prostate, making me almost crouch. Toby caught me, wrapping his arm securely around my waist to keep me standing while my legs started to tremble. His lips touched my earlobe, and my eyes fluttered wide at his words. His low, husky voice echoed through my ears when he whispered, "Undo your pants."

Chapter 22: Coming Out of the Closet

My eyes widened as Toby's grip tightened around my waist, my body stiff as stone.

Did I just hear right? Did Toby — the same guy who told me he was straight — ask me to undo my pants?!

Mrs. Gabs kept moaning louder, which made it even harder for me to concentrate. The warmth of Toby's hand sunk through the fabric of my shirt, and I wanted him to hold me closer to him.

"You know, Jihoon," he murmured. "You've been fidgeting a lot on our way here."

My eyes widened in horror when Toby raised his knee between my legs, making the toy go deeper inside me. A moan almost escaped my throat, but he put his hand over my mouth.

Something tells me he's known for a while.

My face turned red in embarrassment, my ears burning like fire.

"What do you want me to do?" he asked. "Can you hold it in?"

I vigorously shook my head, putting my hand around his arm and lowering his hand from my mouth just enough so that I could speak. But I didn't want him to let go.

"Take it out," I begged. "*Please.*"

I didn't bother having second thoughts. I didn't even feel guilty. My mind was clouded with desire, and my body was itching to be touched. For Hell's sake, I had a ginormous sex toy vibrating inside me and a hot guy was standing right behind me.

How in the world was I supposed to think straight at a time like this?!

When Mrs. Gabs' bed squeaked louder, I took the opportunity to take my belt off and unzip my pants. Toby helped me lower my pants and briefs below my waist, my cock springing out, fully hard.

"Bend forward," whispered Toby, sliding his hand up my back until he reached my shoulder, gently pushing me forward. I did as I was told and bent forward, pulling up my shirt and biting down on the fabric in case I made a noise.

Why did Toby agree to do this? Was he just trying to help out a distressed friend? Maybe he was curious? Moreover, what would Jax think? What was he going to do when he finds out that—

My thoughts were cut off when I felt Toby spread my ass cheeks. I tried to muffle my moan when his fingers reached the area that throbbed, trying to let my knees buckle. I tried concentrating on breathing, but my eyes rolled back when Toby's fingers slipped around the edge, pushing the toy further.

I told myself that as embarrassing as this situation was, all I had to do was cut Toby out of my life afterward and pretend like we had never met. That was what I did whenever I had a one-night stand: cut ties before I got too attached and run back to Jax until he got bored of me.

But for some reason, the idea of not being able to see Toby's radiating smile, to hear him speak my name in his soft voice, and never see his kind eyes again, bothered me.

I took a sharp breath as Toby started pulling the toy out of me, shuddering in pleasure as my tip dripped with precum. But right when I thought he would pull it out completely, he pushed it back in. I yelped from the jolt, synching with Mrs. Gabs' screeches as the man pounded her ass. Toby pulled me towards him and my knees shivered. He held onto me so that I wouldn't crouch completely as he started pulling the vibrator in and out of my anus, each time hitting closer to my prostate. By now, I was panting and breathing loudly, squirming in his grasp while trying my best to stay still. My back arched against his broad chest, and I wrapped my right hand around my aching cock that rubbed against my belly.

"Toby," I whimpered, feeling his hot breath against the nape of my neck as he teased me with the toy. "Fuck," I whimpered, tightening my grip that went faster up and down my length. I was starting to climax, and I felt my entire body shake. Toby pushed the vibrator against my sweet spot. I moaned just as loud as Mrs. Gabs, my body shaking uncontrollably. I started stroking my length, going quicker and quicker and squirting into the palm of my hand. I leaned my forehead against the wall, panting as quietly as I could. My dick was still twitching, juice dripping down the tip and trailing down my shaky thighs.

I tried to find my voice. "That—"

Toby put his hand over my mouth.

"Felt amazing," I heard Mrs. Gabs sigh. "Shit, my husband will be back soon."

"Don't bring up that wretched man's name in front of me," said the man, slapping what I was guessing was Mrs. Gabs' ass. "Say, I might be crazy, but did you hear a voice while we were fucking?"

"Only mine," giggled Mrs. Gabs.

"We should hurry up and leave."

I could hear them put on their clothes. I didn't want them to leave. I'd rather hear them fucking and say cringey things to each other than face Toby right now.

What was I supposed to do? Thank him for helping me jerk off?! And how would I explain why I had a sex toy driven deep inside me? Would he spread rumors at school and tell his friends? Would he find me disgusting like everyone else? No, Toby wasn't like that, was he? He was different. Right?

I tried to keep calm and reassure myself, but the second the two lovers left the room and shut the door, a tortuous silence broke through. As soon as I heard the front door close, I pulled my pants up and quickly stepped out of the closet. I didn't bother turning around to see Toby's face or reaction. I didn't want to. I hurried to the table and grabbed multiple tissues, desperately cleaning my hands to rid myself of my sins. But guilt started to weigh over my shoulders, and I started hating myself for every disgusting thought I had inside the closet. But I didn't regret it.

My hands were trembling while I continued to rub away the opaque liquid, tears forming inside my eyes.

Disgusting, disgusting, disgusting...

I didn't even know why I was crying. I was the one who asked for it, which only made me feel even more confused and pathetic. *Was it because I was embarrassed? Or was it because I was scared Toby would never see me the same?*

Deep down, I already knew the answer.

"Jihoon."

I squeezed my eyes shut, tears escaping the rims.

Please go away. Please let me suffer in peace. Please don't make this any worse than it already is.

I rubbed the tissue against my hand so hard that the thin fabric ripped. My skin was burning a feverish, bright red. I grabbed more tissues, and even if my hands were "clean," I continued to desperately rub.

"Jihoon," repeated Toby, his voice closer than it was the first time he called me. I spun around the second he touched my arm. He took my bright red hand and gently ran a thumb over the red skin. "You're hurting yourself."

Toby frowned when he noticed something. He flipped my hand over and slowly pulled up my sleeve. The purple cuff marks were still there. "Who did this?"

My eyes widened when he pulled my hand to his lips, gently planting a kiss as if to hold the most delicate flower in his hand. His brown eyes then looked into mine. The realization hit me.

"You lied to me," I whispered weakly. "You're not straight, are you?"

"I lied about a few things," he admitted, still holding my hand. "Do you remember when we met in the bar? And I told you that I didn't recognize you?"

I could hardly nod.

"I know it wasn't the first time we'd met. We first met on the bus on our way to the campus." Toby had such a sweet smile. "How could I forget someone so beautiful?"

"Then why did you lie?"

"I didn't want to scare you away. I had a feeling you'd avoid me if I told you I remembered what happened in this bus. And if you knew I liked you, you would have pushed me away."

My eyes widened in shock. "You what?"

Toby pulled me closer to him, wrapping an arm around my waist and looking deep into my eyes with a soft, shy smile. "I like you, Jihoon. Will you go out with me?"

Chapter 23: Choose Me

The words repeated in my head: *"Will you go out with me?"*

Within seconds, my face blushed hot red. My mind screamed at me to react, to do something, breathe, pull my hand away—*anything*! But I stood there, his hand still around mine, his body so close to mine, his face only inches away, his lips, oh his beautiful lips...

Damn it, Jihoon, this isn't the time to get distracted!

"You're blushing," he murmured.

"Of course, I am! You're standing so close."

"Do you want me to step away?"

"No!" I blurted too quickly. Toby laughed at my reaction, only making me even more frustrated, partially because I couldn't help but find his husky laugh so fucking hot.

"If you're going to be this cute, I'll be tempted to kiss you," he murmured, biting his lip as his eyes trailed to mine.

That is not what a straight man is supposed to say!

"Why do you even like me? We hardly know each other."

"You intrigue me."

My mouth went dry. "I am not your eighth-grade science experiment."

"I didn't mean it like that," he chuckled shyly, looking at me with those charming eyes. "I want to get to know you."

"You want to know what's wrong with me?"

He shook his head. "To know who you are."

Since I was a teenager, my entire existence revolved around the few adjectives Jax threw at my face, molding an identity. Without him, who would I be?

"I don't date," I muttered coldly, pulling my hand away from his.

"Is it because of your roommate?"

His question caught me off guard. "There's nothing between Jax and me. I just don't like commitment."

"Is that why you sleep with random men like Mr. Gabs?"

I looked him straight in the eyes despite the burn in my cheeks. "Do you have a problem with that?"

"No, I'm actually flattered," he said with a smile. "The fact that you're so reluctant to accept my feelings proves that I'm different from everyone else."

I quickly tried to find a lie. "It's not like that."

"Then why don't we try dating? I don't mind if you're in it just for the sex. You can use me if you want. You won't have to feel guilty about hurting me if I already know your intentions." He tilted his head with a small smile. "I don't want to boast, but I'm pretty good in bed."

My lips parted as my heart raced like a stallion.

He was right. Why was I so reluctant to be with him? I shouldn't be this scared if he was just like any other guy.

My eyes dropped to the floor, unable to keep eye contact.

I didn't want him to get hurt.

I swallowed hard.

No, you're just afraid of falling in love.

"I'm not a good person," I whispered.

"If your definition of not being a good person is someone who has trust and self-esteem issues because they've been hurt so much, I'll accept it," Toby said calmly. "That doesn't stop me from wanting to be with you."

My chest hurt. Why was my heart racing so fast?

"I'm not pressuring you to do anything, and I don't want to make you uncomfortable. I'm telling you how I feel and what I want. What you do with it is your choice. If you don't want me, I'll accept your decision."

My grip tightened around him immediately, scared he'd leave. "No," I whispered. "I... I want to. I want to try and be with you." I said.

He smiled. "Then can I kiss you?"

My eyes snapped wide open.

"I only asked for a kiss. I'm not asking you to marry me."

Flustered, I said, "Sorry."

"Don't apologize when you've done nothing wrong." He cupped his hand around my jaw, his fingers below my ear, and leaned in for a kiss. At this rate, my heart was beating so fast that I wouldn't be surprised if I had a heart attack. My body naturally leaned closer to his, my lips slowly parting, but my phone rang right before our lips touched.

It was Jax. His number was saved under the name *Jackass*. I was about to answer, but Toby pulled me towards him, my eyes snapping wide open as our lips pressed together. My phone continued to ring in my hand, but Toby's hands slowly wrapped around my waist. As much as I wanted to continue the kiss, my mind flashbacked to the last time I didn't answer Jax's call, and I pulled away once again, pressing one hand against Toby's chest to stop him.

"I need to answer this," I whispered. I turned around to answer, but Toby rested his chin on my shoulder, wrapping his arms around me. His hair tickled my neck, sending goosebumps down my arms. I tried to ignore him, but he suddenly nibbled on my earlobe, and I almost dropped my phone with a yelp.

"Is it important?"

All I could manage was a strained "yes."

The phone continued to ring, and I knew I only had a few seconds to answer.

"Don't," he rasped, pressing his forehead against my shoulder. "If we're going to be together, I want us to be exclusive."

He kissed me again. This time, I didn't resist. My heart thudded heavily against my chest, and the phone stopped buzzing. I pushed away the thoughts of Jax and all the consequences I'd suffer later. No matter how painful it'd be, this kiss was worth it. I opened my mouth, letting Toby's tongue slip into mine to deepen the kiss, hands lost in his lustrous brown hair. My back arched at his warmth, and I felt drugged by his touch.

Fuck, this boy can kiss.

When he pulled away, he rested his forehead against mine, looking at me with those forest-brown eyes. He gave me a smile that strung a cord in my heart.

"Jihoon." Toby whispered my name, his low, husky voice forming my name in that cute little accent of his had me dying, and I felt like I had lost my goddamn mind. "Choose me."

Chapter 24: Jax 3, Jihoon 0

I got off the bus and entered the building to my apartment in a daze. When the elevator doors closed in front of me, I stood in the metal box, staring at the silver doors without a thought in mind. I watched the dull orange number shift as I went past each floor. And then it hit me. Everything hit me like a train going at full speed.

Someone kissed me. Toby kissed me. Toby *likes* me.

I was so bewildered that I had forgotten that we didn't manage to find the illegal footage in Mr. Gabs' house. Once his wife left, we looked everywhere, but it was nowhere to be found. Aside from that, someone *liked* me. A real human being. A normal person was interested in disgusting little me. *Did this mean I have a boyfriend now? That I'm in a relationship? Can I do normal things with my significant other? Go on dates and have fun?*

I'd slept with countless men, but I'd dated none.

I raised my hand to my lips and brushed the tip of my index against the area that touched Toby's lips, contemplating as they still felt warm, as if his lips had never left mine. I wish they never did. I snapped out of my thoughts when I heard the loud *ding*.

I was home.

I reluctantly trudged out of the elevator and slid the key into the keyhole, twisting the door open. Jax's slippers were still in the shoe rack, which meant he wasn't home. I let out a small sigh of relief, removing my shoes and putting on my slippers. Jax was probably still at work. I'd have enough time to grab some clothes and ask Toby if I could stay at his place. I shook my head at the intruding thought.

No, you don't want to come off as too clingy.

I paused. *Maybe I can crash at someone else's place? Would that upset Toby? Will he think I'm cheating on him?*

Inexperienced in dating, I suddenly felt confused and lost. How did relationships even work? The furthest I'd gone with a man was to his bed. Feelings were never involved unless it was with Jax, and even then, it was one-sided.

Speaking of Jax, I didn't want to know what he'd do to me after ignoring his call. He would definitely leave a bruise or two for taking the vibrator out. I needed to get out of here while I still could. I walked down the hall but stopped when I heard a squeaking noise coming from my room.

Was there a mouse in the house?

As much as I wanted to believe it was a mouse, the noise was too loud. As I got closer, I could hear mutters and whispers. I approached my room and could see Jax through the small crack of the half-closed door and Madison below him. She was naked, her long, slim legs wide open for him, while Jax thrust inside her. I was mortified.

They were having sex in my bed.

"Harder," moaned Madison, her entire body shaking in sync at each thrust. My stomach lurched at the sight of Jax making love to someone else, and I could feel my face turning as white as a sheet of paper. "Harder!"

I didn't know why I felt like vomiting. I felt completely fine seeing Mrs. Gabs making love to another man. By *fine*, I meant not nauseous. But now, I felt like the walls were closing in on me. Waves of nausea added to my misery. I needed to get out of here.

But the second I stepped back, the floor below me creaked beneath my weight, and Jax's eyes flickered up. His bright blue eyes locked with mine. A small smirk formed at the tip of his lips. His eyes were so blue that I felt seasick as if the orbs were swallowing me whole.

"Hey, Madison," he started, raising her left leg over his shoulder. Beads of sweat rolled down his smooth skin. He called her name while looking at me. "

"Ngh," was all the poor thing could answer.

"What do you think about us having sex in my roommate's room?" he asked, making me flinch when he wouldn't even say my name. I was reduced to 'roommate.' That was all I was to him. All I ever was to him. "You think he'd be mad if I made you cum all over his sheets?"

My knees started to feel weak, and I clutched my stomach.

"Don't, ngh, don't talk about him," she whimpered. "You're always, ah, you're always talking about him."

My eyes widened at her words, and I watched her stretch out her arms and wrap them around Jax, hugging him closer to her. It was as if she was taking something that was mine right under my nose, and I couldn't do anything about it.

"Do I?" chuckled Jax, eyes still on me. "Does it make you jealous?" to which she moaned, "Yes!"

Jax grinned, slamming harder into her. The sound of their bodies slapping made it unbearable for me to watch, and yet I stood there, frozen stiff, staring. I took another step back, but Jax's eyes narrowed, and I knew he was ordering me to stay. He knew what he was doing and loved every second of it. He wanted to see me crumble and suffer.

"Do you want me to leave him?" he asked. "How about I live with you, Maddie?" He thrust harder into her, and she screamed, crying Jax's name, making me hate everything that much more.

~~I wanted to be the one under Jax.~~
~~I wanted to be the one holding him.~~
~~I wanted to be the one Jax was making love to.~~
~~I wanted Jax.~~
I needed to leave.

"We'd have as much sex as you'd want," he went on blissfully.

"No," I whispered, shaking my head.

131

"I'd fuck you every day." He grinned, making me shake my head even harder as tears filled my eyes. "I'd leave him, and he'd be alone in this house."

"Jax," Madison and I said simultaneously, but her voice overpowered mine, leaving me unheard. "I love you, Jax. I love you so much!"

My eyes widened as she pushed her lips against Jax's, and when he lowered his gaze and broke eye contact with me, I felt like my whole world crashed into flames. Their bodies moved in perfect harmony; they looked beautiful together as if they were meant to be. Even bare naked, they were beautiful.

I could already envision their future.Jax would marry Madison, and he'd move out. He'd leave me, and I'd be alone. I'd be alone like in high school, alone like I'd been my entire life.

I took a step forward, but Jax raised his head, and our eyes met again. A smug smile was drawn on his face. He was grinning so widely as if he'd won the lottery and was at the peak of ecstasy.

"I love you too."

With one last thrust, Madison let out a piercing scream, nails scratching down Jax's back while her body shook. When he pulled out of her, he tossed the condom with the rest of the pile on the floor. While Madison tried to catch her breath, Jax stood up and walked towards me without breaking eye contact. Each footfall grew louder and louder, each thud pounding into my eardrums, adrenaline pumping through my veins. We were now only a few inches away, his shadow casting over my body. His silky blond hair was a beautiful mess, and his distinct cheekbones and angular jaw made him look devilishly handsome.

I wanted him.

"Jax," I stammered, my trembling hand reaching out to fulfill my desire. He smiled at me, but the door slammed in my face before my hand could reach him. The echo of the door rang through my ears.

"Why did you close the door?" I could hear Madison's muffled voice.

"There was an annoying breeze outside," Jax replied. "It's fine. It should be gone by now."

Translation: *I don't need you anymore. Leave.*

Chapter 25: Fireworks

I somehow managed to get to Toby's house. He pushed me onto his bed and pressed his lips against mine while unbuttoning my wet shirt that stuck to my skin. I had run here under the pouring rain. As soon as Jax closed the door on me, I left in a rush and didn't bother to grab an umbrella. Toby threw my clothes aside before taking off his own. He placed his palm on my torso, and I bit my lip at the warmth of his touch.

"Are you nervous?" he asked.

I stared at him through my wet bangs, forcing a smile, pretending I was okay when I clearly wasn't.

Jax was with another girl—it was nothing new to me. It wasn't like I didn't know about Madison. It had never been a secret. But the cold, distant look in his eyes and the way he closed the door in my face without a trace of remorse or hesitation hurt me. It hurt so much that I needed something to numb the pain. I needed *someone* to numb it for me.

"Don't treat me like a virgin," I muttered coldly. "You're not the first man I've slept with."

I didn't really care if what I said hurt Toby. I didn't care if he saw me as a prostitute, a man slut, or any of the insults people had thrown at me since I was a kid. I was no better than any of the above.

"Then why is your body so tense?" Toby asked, touching my tightened stomach. "Relax, I won't hurt you."

But I wanted him to hurt me. I wanted him to make me suffer and remind me that I was a piece of trash who wasn't worth anything. His right hand gently cupped my cheek, brushing over my lips.

"Don't make that face."

"What face?"

"The one you make when you're about to cry," he whispered.

Toby kissed me, his tongue sliding into my mouth. My arms wrapped around his strong neck, and I could hear him unbuckle his belt. I felt his bulge pressing against my thigh, and my eyes widened.

"You're hard," I breathed.

"I couldn't stop thinking about you since this morning," he admitted, brushing a wet lock of hair clumped on my forehead. "Did your roommate hurt you again?"

I looked away, but he pulled my chin towards him. "It's fine," he said, locking eyes with me. "I told you you could use me."

His fingers brushed over my erect nipples. I flinched at the touch, and he smiled.

"You're sensitive here," he murmured curiously, making my cheeks burn red.

"No, I'm—"

He lowered his head and sucked my left nipple. My back arched; hands tangled in his hair as he rolled the hard bead over his tongue. My breathing got louder as he sucked harder and gasped when he nibbled on it with his front teeth.

"Toby," I moaned, but he continued to slurp and suck while grinding against my thigh. My lower body got excited by the taste of his tongue and the smell of fresh pine on his skin. I had a feeling this wasn't his first time either. I pushed him onto his back and got on top of him, lowering his pants and briefs down his waist to give him head. But my lips parted in shock as his erection sprung out of the fabric. I expected him to be big but didn't think he'd be this huge. He was as big as Jax.

I looked up at Toby with a gulp, and he grinned.

"You look flustered," he noted.

I tried to keep a straight face, but it obviously wasn't working.

"If you can't—"

"I can," I insisted hastily. *I can do this.*

He sat up as I got on my knees. I kissed his tip while he caressed my hair. I opened my mouth and took him in, encouraged by the deep grunt of his voice. I lowered my head and started bobbing up and down before stopping at the tip to suck on the slit of his dick, sliding my tongue around it like a lollipop.

"Fuck," he hissed, throwing his head back.

When his erection was covered in my saliva, I kissed down the side before taking him whole, and this time, as deep as I could. His size widened my throat, and he moaned in arousal. I could taste his precum fill my mouth. My jaw hurt, and I pulled away. *He tasted sweet.*

"You're thinking of someone else," growled Toby, roughly pushing me onto my back.

I looked at him. "What if I am?"

He slammed his lips against mine, pulling away only to growl, "Focus on me."

My cock twitched at his command. Nice guy Toby was hot, but his possessive and jealous side was *sexy.* He pulled down my pants and bent my knees towards my chest before lowering himself to suck on my asshole.

"Wait," I stuttered, cut off by a moan. This was way too embarrassing.

I gasped as I felt his tongue poke inside my hole. I put my hand over my mouth to stop my moans, but Toby lowered my arms and intertwined his fingers around mine.

"I'd rather hear you make noises," he chuckled, kissing my sensitive inner thigh. "That way, I know it feels good."

But I knew Toby didn't need to hear me moan to know he had skills. He flipped me onto my stomach, and I could hear him rummage for something in his drawer. It was a condom, the same brand and size Jax used. I got on my knees and arched my back, letting him use the saliva coated around my ass to slip two fingers in. I swore under my breath, hearing the squelching noise of his fingers pushing in and out of my asshole. My back arched even more as he pushed in a third finger, making it impossible for me to retain any noise. My cock was so erect that the tip touched my stomach, dripping wet.

"Put it in," I begged, turning my head around and meeting Toby's gaze. "I want you in me."

Toby's eyes widened at my plea. He ripped open the condom and slipped his erection in, spreading my cheeks and inserting it into me. Jax would have slammed into me right away. Every time he did, something inside me would rip from the unexpected brutality, often causing me to bleed. Of course, that didn't stop Jax from pounding into my ass. But Toby was different. He was careful and gentle, and each movement was affectionate. He held onto my hips and slowly pushed in. It felt nice to be treated like a human.

"Tell me if it hurts," he said.

"I'm fine," I winced through gritted teeth.

"I'm only halfway in, Jihoon."

My jaw dropped in surprise. Toby pushed the rest of his dick inside me, and I gasped, feeling like it filled my insides.

"Fuck," he muttered. "You said you weren't a virgin, but you're so tight."

He thrust deeper inside of me, and I cried. He pulled me up and wrapped his arms around my chest, thrusting into me quicker. The bed squeaked as our bodies moved in perfect synch, our voices ragged as we moaned from pleasure. His thrusts grew quick, going deeper and deeper inside of me.

"Toby," I moaned as he slammed into me. He flipped me onto my back and lowered his head, kissing me while thrusting. Everything felt amazing.

No, it felt *fantastic*.

I lowered my hand to jerk off, but Toby stopped me and pinned my hands over my head.

"Bear with me a little longer," he panted. But I was already reaching my limit, my erection twitching, begging to cum. I moaned as he went harder, the sound of his body slapping against my butt cheeks echoing inside the room.

Unable to hold it in, I squirted all over myself. Cum projected out of my tip and to my chest and stomach as my erection twitched. My body continued to tremble from the orgasm as I panted for breath.

Toby removed the condom and jerked himself off, squirting all over me. He wiped it with his hand before pressing his fingers between the seam of my lips. I stared at him but widened my mouth, licking the opaque liquid off his fingers.

"Was I too rough?" he asked. I shook my head. "Then I hope you're reading for another round."

We continued to have sex until our bodies ached and felt sore. It felt weird. Sex didn't feel like just sex. It wasn't empty feelings and a simple desire for pleasure. It felt as if there was something more than just two bodies trying to orgasm. It was dark and rainy outside, but I felt warm inside. As Toby continued thrusting inside me while I screamed his name, I closed my eyes and saw fire color.

Chapter 26: 3 a.m.

It was three a.m. when I woke up beside Toby. He was asleep, wearing nothing but his boxers. I slowly sat up, careful not to wake him. Without any particular reason, I looked at him and smiled. Something about him lit a fire in my heart and warmed my soul, something that I had never felt with Jax. With Jax… Everything was cold. I didn't know how to describe it, but I never felt safe in his arms or found true warmth—only temporary comfort.

I studied Toby's sharp jaw and chin, the curve of his high cheekbones, and his closed lids that hid two blazing hazel eyes deep in slumber. His strong chest raised and fell slowly at each breath, and I wanted to rest my head against it and fall back asleep in his arms. But the rain outside that hit against the window caught my attention. It was almost pitch dark outside.

I slowly got out of the covers and tiptoed towards the closed window, pressing my fingers against the transparent glass. The heat of my body created a fog that expanded slowly. I watched the rain dribble down one by one, wanting to open the window to touch them. I wanted to feel the cool autumn breeze against my cheeks and the cold raindrops against my skin, smell the fragrance of earth entering my nostrils, and fill my body with a sweet sense of joy.

I grabbed my clothes that were laid across the floor, surprised that my body was moving so flexibly after the number of times Toby and I went at it last night. My body hurt, but the pain I felt with Jax was incomparable. This? This was nothing. Toby was careful and cautious with me the entire time. He treated me the way I should have been treated years ago, the way Jax never did and probably never would.

Yesterday was blissful. It was what I imagined sex to be when I was a teenager. It was what a lot of people believed sex to be when they were young and naïve: passionate, full of pleasure and desire, two bodies and souls linked harmoniously.

I put on my shoes and quickly tied the laces before heading towards the door. I stopped for a second and turned around to look at Tobias, who slept peacefully under the covers. Even though he was asleep, I smiled at him before leaving his dorm room to go outside.

I walked down the dark halls, and the sound of rain pounding against the windows made them clatter violently. The further I went, the darker and colder the atmosphere seemed. The memories of Jax and I in high school, the memories of us after graduation, every trace of him filled my mind like water rushing into an empty tank.

I could still remember how I stared at him from afar, watching him play football with his friends; how he'd look up from the field and meet my eyes as if he knew I'd been staring from the class window the entire time. He'd smile at me, his lips almost touching the blues of his eyes like a child reaching up to touch the sky, starting fireworks inside my chest. At moments like these, he was different. It felt like he showed me a side of him that he kept secret from the rest of the world, a glimpse of him only I was allowed to see. It was me and Jax, no one else, and that feeling made me feel invincible.

I could still remember how he used to bully me in front of his friends, becoming an unrecognizable persona, barking racist and homophobic slurs and telling me that I was disgusting for who I was. They'd steal my lunch money to buy cigarettes, copy off my homework to get better grades, beat me until I couldn't stand, and

whatever they did, they made me believe it was my fault until I
believed them.

I always blamed myself and wondered why I was born like
this and not like them. Why couldn't I be like the other kids? Was
it my gender? My race? My sexuality? Or was it just… Me?

But every time I was on the verge of losing my mind, Jax was
there. And that was the problem. He was *always* there. I strongly
believed that life was always about timing. And time played in his
favor and against mine. He was there when I was at my lowest.
He'd give out his hand and tell me things would be okay. He
hugged me behind closed doors and told me I shouldn't be sad,
that I was important and meant something to him. To *someone*.

The pounding of the rain got louder, and I quickened my pace
as I started getting closer to the exit, gulping as I felt a lump in my
throat. The memories continued to flood my mind.

I still remember the day I tried to kill myself, standing on the
school's rooftop, and Jax said words I could never forget.

"I'd miss you if you went."

His words could have been shallow lies, but they meant the
world to me. They gave me a reason to live. It was the same way
politicians would tell tired, weary soldiers the glory and victory
they'd achieve at the end of the war, only to be thrown deeper into
the abyss. They were nothing but lies, but those lies gave us hope.
It gave us a reason to live.

"For the first time in your life, you're actually wanted."

Jax gave me a sense of belonging.

But it was over now. I was tired of being a victim, tired of his
games, tired of being his puppet, tired of getting hurt over and over
again, hoping and wishing that somehow, in that twisted mind of
his, he'd actually cared for me, that somewhere in that cruel, cold
heart of his, he might actually have feelings for me. I had to face
the truth. We weren't lovers. My feelings and attachment meant
nothing to him. In spite of the bittersweet moments we shared, he
never truly cared for me.

"Do you love him?"

I pushed open the doors and smiled as the cold breeze brushed against my cheeks, smiling widely as I saw the rain.

Jax made my heart drop and my stomach ache. One day he would make me feel like the happiest man on earth. Other times, he made me feel like I was about to lose my mind. And I knew that leaving him was going to hurt. It was going to hurt like hell. I had given him everything, but it wasn't enough. But it would things would eventually get better, and I'd move on with the scars he left. My world would no longer revolve around a toxic man that never had the heart to spare me a glance. And that was the saddest part.

You spent your entire life trying to please someone, only to lose yourself and get hurt in the end.

I felt the rain pour against my head and continued walking forward. Within seconds, I was soaked in water, my bangs stuck to my forehead and drooped over my eyes, hanging in clumps. I was shivering, goosebumps trailing down my arms and spine. It was cold to the point where I felt numb, but I liked it.

I ran down the campus, smiling widely as I heard the quenching noises of the puddles below my feet bring back nostalgic memories of when I was a kid. It had been a while since I felt so free, so alone, but free. Anyone who saw me would probably think I was crazy, running in the rain while laughing like a maniac, but I didn't care. For once in my life, I didn't care.

When I was out of breath, I stopped in the middle of the campus, a few giggles escaping my hoarse throat. My head tilted back, and I looked up, feeling the gentle kisses of the rain, my vision turning into a blur. My eyes squinted, staring at the darkness of the empty, pitch-black sky.

A smile spread across my face as I took a deep breath, smelling the autumn's fresh dew. And I closed my eyes.

I'm free.

Author's Note

Book 2 of My Lovely Roommate will be published in the upcoming months! Please don't hesitate to follow me on my socials @letsgohomehidee to stay tuned. It would also mean a lot if you could leave a review on Amazon. I would love to know your thoughts and comments on the story.

I.J Hidee

Made in United States
North Haven, CT
17 December 2024